# HOW DO YOU STOP A MAGPIE MOBBING YOUR MIND?

E. K. J. WRIGHT

The Book Guild Ltd

First published in Great Britain in 2021 by
The Book Guild Ltd
9 Priory Business Park
Wistow Road, Kibworth
Leicestershire, LE8 0RX
Freephone: 0800 999 2982
www.bookguild.co.uk
Email: info@bookguild.co.uk
Twitter: @bookguild

Typeset in 10pt Minion Pro

Printed and bound in the UK by TJ Books LTD, Padstow, Cornwall


ISBN 978 1913913 199


British Library Cataloguing in Publication Data.
A catalogue record for this book is available from the British Library.

Dedicated to Andrew, Oscar and Laurie,
loyal companions through life's noise

'We all want quiet. We all want beauty... We all need space. Unless we have it, we cannot reach that sense of quiet in which whispers of better things come to us gently.'

# CONTENTS

Beggar's Well

Sweet Chestnut Avenue

Socknersh Manor

Glydwish Farm

Stallionback Field

The Bellington-Fraser Folly

Magical Beech Tree

Trolliloes Forest

River Washwell

Hilaire and Colette's Golden Joydle

Cervine Centre Field

Pheasant Fields

CHAPTER 1

# ONE FOR SORROW

L
ife's soundtrack had stopped until the day we came to Heartsease. Since Dad's death, the magpie had descended, drowning out each and every joyous lilting lyric. The empty void had merely been punctuated with rasping dirge-like dissonance: the 5am alarm clock of traffic rumble, the furtive pit-pat of Mum's bathroom jogging, and the doleful wail of an ambulance siren echoing that traumatic day.

But the first tranquil moments in our new Arcadia had roused my deafened ears to nature's rapturous rhythm. The soothing baseline of the rising and falling breeze, the pizzicato trill of birdsong, all crescendoing in the distant 'Kee-ow' of a soaring buzzard.

Like a glinting viridine gemstone, the view had enticed Dad to Heartsease. The whale-backed Washwell Valley had evoked the halcyon wooded hills of his Devon childhood. For Mum, the ocean-green undulations had conjured up our ozone-infused Augusts of exploration. And I saw a girl slumbering in the rosy gloam, her sylvan corkscrew curls cascading down the steep-sided ravine.

On our first visit, Dad had pinpointed a lone tree atop the furthest ridge, spotlit by the celestial shimmer of the lustrous, smouldering sun. We'd imagined all the thrilling adventures that lay between us and it. Dad had even bought a brand new OS Explorer map in anticipation.

Bristling with resentment, the car-brake splutter of a startled pheasant jolted me back to my less than radiant reality. Mum was in full-blown silent automaton mode, hurriedly heaving the final packing boxes one by one from the boot to the back door. My desperate offers of help were fiercely barked down, as if she was condemned to her downtrodden destiny.

Now completely oblivious to the seafoam-flecked scenery, her first round of self-punishment culminated in a purposeless route-march round the garden. With a hefty door bang as her parting pronouncement, she swiftly scuttled off to her unpacking penance.

Flustered, headstrong Mum would need time to decompress after her self-inflicted thrashing, so I perched on the warm brick wall and attempted to lose myself in the pink and blue coconut ice twilight. But a great tit's metronome chant of 'teatime, teatime' was an insistent countdown to the impending meal. I knew she would need support and instantly dreaded the morass of tagliatelle tiffs and exhausting excuses which lay before me. Plagued by nauseating uneasiness, I was reminded of the other avian foe in my life…

Until that seismic afternoon, I'd been blind to the asphyxiating corvine stranglehold that was gripping me. It was four months since Dad's heart attack and intoxicating angst now permeated every single brick of 17 Durrington Gardens. The summer holidays were usually crammed with gleeful promise, but now the days dragged drearily towards the imminent move without my beloved idol.

I'd felt the first rumbling tremors at breakfast's pancake-tower palaver. Liberally drizzling the gargantuan stack with maple syrup, Mum had promptly announced that her tummy was gripey and she wasn't feeling very hungry. She instead opted to make a meal of the washing-up, assuring me that she'd whip up a storm at lunch 'to make up for it'. Leaving me to devour the skyscraper of scrumptiousness, she headed out for her ever-lengthening run in faded bobbly gym wear.

Although always a Daddy's girl at heart, it was nevertheless agonising to witness Mum's ritualistic self-abuse. She was clearly not 'fine', as she put it, but my suggestion of the GP had been snappishly brushed off. Her spindly legs now resembled her low-carb cantaloupe melon 'indulgence' of choice. She seemed to be getting an awful lot of things in her drained scarlet-smeared fawn's eyes. And surely mums were normally apple or pear not lollipop-shaped?

Yes, we'd been relentlessly hounded by a pesky ingratiating gatecrasher these past months. But unlike the impromptu visits of Dad's my-head's-bigger-than-yours cousin Margot, there was no prospect of a life-saving bus home. What's more, I was utterly powerless to turf this troublesome trespasser out of our lives.

Numbed by my jim-jams, I decided to lessen Mum's laundry load by having a pyjama day. It was too much effort to shower anyway. And why open the curtains? My besieged brain saw them as a reassuringly impenetrable shield against the battering ram of the outside world.

So I spent a morning of lingering wistful fug failing to pack up my things ready for the move. That was after wasting half an hour trying to find meaning on the squares of Instagram. 'Be ruthless!' Mum had snarled. But I was incapable of chucking treasured glimpses of Dad into a black bin bag. My tormented eyes pricked with stinging sharp teardrops at the discovery of *The Jungle Book* DVD. I remembered how Dad had jived around the living room as crazily as King Louie himself, his spirited flat singing strangling the soundtrack. I longed once again to hear his own unique Bagheera and his fearless Shere Khan, cuddled up together under my safari-print tepee.

The spring of tears bubbled over into a raging unquenchable torrent when I unearthed my dog-eared nature books. Dad had been wasted to management consultancy. The most generous legacy he'd given me was his passion for our natural history. 'The world is yours to explore' was one of his favourite phrases. The excitement had mounted with each school day that passed counting down to our weekends as 'intrepid explorers'. I had never met anybody who could get so enthusiastic about reproduction in hermaphroditic leeches. Or instantly recognise the popping corn-chirrups of a house martin. Or point out the viper's bugloss and sea-spurrey en route to a secret rock pool. The devastating tornado of his death, however, had flattened any of my budding zoologist aspirations, or indeed *any* interest in anything at all.

I leafed through the familiar comforting pages of *The Book of Country and Seashore Life* and drank in their consoling musty smell. Stumbling upon '*This book belongs to Ella Pearson*' scrawled in Dad's spidery handwriting on the frontispiece forced me to stop. Which was just as well, given that my face was a searing sodden chilli-ripple smear of rancour and I didn't want to be another burden on Mum's horsewhipped raw-boned back.

With three weeks to go until the move, I'd achieved precisely nothing and felt as useless as our empty biscuit barrel. In my self-consumed and apathetic state, I'd even neglected to check on the falcon…

Amidst the raw shattered blur of the day following Dad's death, a tiny pinprick of hope had tried to peek through. An impossible knot of sorrow and confusion, I was a helpless bystander on the dire situation unfurling before me. A leaden chainmail of lament weighed me down at every torpid turn. If God existed, then how had He let this happen?

The endless flurry of concerned yet insincere answer phone messages: 'We're so sorry for your loss, Jenna, if there's anything at all that we can do…' throbbed in my Piccadilly Circus-head. Mum had self-quarantined with heartbreak and was being nursed by ever-tactful Granny. I suddenly felt as lonely as the Ténéré Tree. Not being an adult didn't mean I wasn't hurting too! Thirsting to escape my own Saharan desolation, I fled to the roof terrace like a quaking lonesome jerboa.

Durrington Gardens and identikit Brightling Tower next door were ill-named solemn ravens guarding Albion Road. Their depressing drab façades had imbued the apartments with an irrepressible melancholy. In the excuse for a communal garden, a solitary withering tree was being strangled by a boa constrictor of ivy, and the weathered bench was so unyielding that nobody ever sat on it.

Our meagre patch of freedom had been the one and only benefit of living in the penthouse flat. Dad and I had shared many a heart-to-heart up on the roof terrace whilst tending to our pots of tomatoes and begonias. All the same, after ten years of weathering the suburban straggle of South Wickham, Dad's countryside roots had craved natural nourishment. Heartsease was the rural paradise he'd always hungered after. How cruel that he'd been denied his last supper!

Still throttled by a ligature of despair, I gratefully gulped in the unfettering fresh air at the summit. Curling up in Dad's hammock-cocoon, I wept into his sweet scent. Coming up for breath, my burning sleep-deprived eyes were blinded by a bolt from the lugubrious blue. A pair of scintillating obsidian jewels were staring me out from the adjacent rooftop. Was I hallucinating? Perching on an abandoned window box and wearing a regal cape of ginger ermine and velvety hematite, was a peregrine falcon.

The urban wilderness had become a fertile nesting ground for raptors – Dad and I had even seen peregrines from the Tate Modern's viewpoint, swooping full tilt like anchors hurled from a ship. It was, however, miraculous that the heaven-sent black-moustachioed confidant enthroned metres away from me had been Dad's favourite bird. He had worshipped them as a kid – Nana had even crocheted him a cuddly toy version. Crippled by his non-existent self-esteem, Dad had invariably cowered 'below stairs' as the humble stooge. Perhaps in adopting the lightning-fast falcon as his animal hero, he'd aspired to reach the noble heights of his peerless plumed paragon. He'd explained to me that peregrine meant 'wanderer' and I understood instantly why my starry-eyed dreamer could relate to this agile and inquisitive bird, so frequently was his mind captivated by its next flight of fancy.

And so it was that the falcon became my salvation, a yearned-for trapdoor in the oppressive basement prison of my thoughts. Every day thereafter, I'd found great solace in checking on it, as if I was connecting once again with a tiny shimmering spark of Dad's spirit. Even on the worst of those maudlin moping mackerel's-too-fatty days, its insistent 'there-there' call was a cheering consolation. Sometimes it was there and sometimes it wasn't, but it was a gleaming golden primrose in my wintry woe-ridden world. That was until the realisation of another feathered invader in my life…

Mum returned high on endorphins, her hair shackled by a headband and scragged back in a perfectly smooth ponytail. But the fizzy slick shell belied her erupting-Krakatoa mind. With a great deal of hustle and bustle, she dashed around as if on roller-skates attempting to prepare a simple risotto. Her taut elastic band-limbs near to snapping point, I tried to engage her in anodyne conversation, but could see that her agitated brain was clearly elsewhere.

After the whole convoluted debacle, lunch or, in Mum's case, a lack of it, was served. She still wasn't feeling well and scurried off to fret over the 'packing mountain', promising that she'd have a 'really good' dinner. So I sat alone at the kitchen table, frustratedly pushing the seemingly growing termite-nest of rice around my plate. Paralysing prickles of excruciating anxiety pulsed through each cell of my body, but I didn't want to distress my conscientious no-carbs-for-me cook further by my sudden lack of appetite. Forcing the last few cloying mouthfuls down, I bugged out to the fortifying roof terrace with my phone as an indifferent companion.

Still shuddering from the lunch shenanigans, a flutter of lapis lazuli diverted my distraught rheumy eyes. A silken jade tail followed, accompanied by a rattling cackle. The sound taunted my friendless ears and was unmistakeable. Acclimatising to the clammy outside world, my dazed eyes focused on a scrap of piebald patchwork rummaging in the sunflowers. My magpie nemesis.

'One for sorrow', that was the rhyme, wasn't it? *Everything* was black and white since Dad had died. One minute he was here, and the next he had gone. One day my big dipper-brain was high up, the next it was at rock bottom. I recalled the contentious old wives' tale that magpies steal shiny objects. This pied persecutor of my mind had robbed my shattered soul, snaffled any gram of happiness and was now arrogantly laughing at me for the chaotic mess I'd become.

And what was it doing rifling through Dad's lovingly nurtured plants? As it hopped off, I realised that it was clutching something in its spiteful bill. And then came the rock-wrenching realisation that Mum and I risked being engulfed in a landslide of anguish. Taking a closer look, I saw an uneaten sandwich half-buried in the soil and on careful inspection, another. In all I must have unearthed at least a dozen stark reminders that Mum was seriously unwell.

The more ill Mum had become, the more my inner mournful magpie had feasted and fattened. This corvine kleptomaniac had barricaded my brimming brain to anything which might unmask its balaclava and assuage my suffering.

And now I spotted an eager accomplice to its thievery taking poor Mr. Radmore from Flat 2 for a strenuous walk. Suddenly the potent aftershock struck me that Mum's canine chastiser was a guileful greyhound. With its winkle-picker head and corrugated ribs *this* was the grim spectre that had come to haunt us. As it put its raddled panting owner through his paces, I recognised the detached disdainful look of Mum in its keen eyes. I empathised with the snubbed chihuahua on the opposite pavement, so challenging had it been to communicate with Mum in the past weeks.

My phone even reliably informed me that a group of greyhounds was known as a 'leash'. That sounded about right as I thought of Mum, controlled and restricted in every way by her dogged adversary. I fantasised momentarily that the peregrine would lunge down and gobble up my odious pied oppressor and scare off Mum's heinous hellhound with one of its 200mph crash-dives. The falcon had restored my faith that it could be a fresh beginning for us in the Sussex countryside. But would our tormentors be stowing away in the luggage? As I spied Mum heading out for yet another gruelling pointless run, I wasn't so sure…

The babbling stream-ditty of an upbeat wren startled me back to our hope-filled Heartsease haven. For a bird as minute as my index finger it certainly had a strong set of lungs! It seemed to be imploring me to open my grief-clogged ears to the whispers of the Washwell and let in the joy once more. I pined for the unbridled delight of that mini-maestro. Could Heartsease be my healer?

Glimpsing Mum's darting birdlike eyes and willowy heron-legs buckle under the strain of a chock-full packing box was my urgent cue that she too needed help to fly. A fusillade of concerns peppered my jittery head. Would there be pasta portion quibbles at dinner? Would she allow her tortured, dog-tired body to try out our snug new sofa this evening? She'd promised a 'clean slate' and had even daringly bought a chocolate and cherry ice cream for us to enjoy for pudding. Together, I hoped. Reluctant to part with my rekindled landscape crush, I ached to melt into its balmy, blushing embrace.

CHAPTER 2

# TWO FOR JOY?

A symphony of chirping jubilation had been the 4am wake-up fanfare to my adventure at Heartsease. Snuggled up in my new bed, I had reacquainted my ears with old avian friends and marvelled at the beaming sunlight-ballerinas pirouetting across my duvet. A wood pigeon's emphatic 'come-out-side-El-la' coo had tried to beckon me into the garden. A twittering goldfinch had agreed wholeheartedly with its rapid-fire ping-pong match of song.

I'd heeded their advice. It was necessary after the slight skirmish with Mum regarding how many handfuls of bran flakes she was having for breakfast. Still, at least she'd had something, albeit with a thimbleful of skimmed milk and a great deal of coaxing on my part. I took it as progress. She'd even called me darling, which she hadn't done for ages. Leaving her hefting around some flat-pack furniture, I'd eloped into our little Eden, desperately hoping that we could rebuild our lives as straightforwardly as assembling an IKEA bookcase.

Heartsease was nestled at the centre of our half-acre of wild Sussex, its avocado weatherboard jacket infusing the bungalow with the essence of the greenery beyond. Topped with a checked liquorice-slate cap and wrapped in a speckled scarf of mature trees and wildflowers, it watched over the dramas of the Washwell Valley. It was as if we were melded to the landscape, separated only by a braid of squat beech hedging.

Each plant formed a tile in our mosaic of fecundity. There was a broom-like butterfly bush dusted in purple panicles. Spanning the bark chip path which meandered to our porch was a Chinese bean tree covered in a cerise doily of blossom. Dapples of brilliance glinted through the green lacy veil of a silver birch bride. All finished off with a sprinkle of flowering vermicelli in the overgrown lawn.

Dad's favourite tree had been a small oak tucked at the very back of the sloped haven. It was the perfect lookout tower on life in our vibrant vale of nirvana. We'd had plans to house a nest box in its rugged branches; Dad had even ordered one from the RSPB. But now I'd have to erect it in his memory. Alone.

Feeling a collar of woe tightening around my quivering throat, I suddenly had the urge to climb into its welcoming arms. Cradled in its rhino skin-boughs and sheltered by its lobed lime cellophane canopy, I unshackled my grief and wept into the blissful quiet.

My exhausted brain throbbed with pangs of gnawing sorrow, but nature's tranquillity helped soothe my inner commotion. The laid-back lilt of a whistling blackbird provided a mellow interlude.

The hum of life was abruptly shattered by the drone of Mum's manic hoovering, signalling that it was time for lunch before she went into 'hangry zombie' mode. I hadn't even had the chance to venture out of our gate into the wide wilderness. That would be my reward for enduring the 'how much butter' battle and 'I'm too full for pudding' clash looming before me. Grudgingly I schlepped in, garnering all my strength for the upcoming onslaught.

*

I'd never understood why 'feeling blue' was associated with being glum. With the sky this intensely azure, how was it possible to recollect anything other than happy memories? Radiant cerulean-tinged summer holidays spent searching for elusive red squirrels on magical Brownsea Island, and building life-sized sand cars on Devon beaches.

But regretfully my magpie was my prophet of doom. Today there had certainly been some black and white mealtime-flutters given the strain of Mum's antics. Armed with Dad's OS map and kitted out in my trusty walking boots, I'd retreated to the Unexplored. Would I reach Dad's famed tree on the far side of the valley?

Closing the gate behind me and feeling like a fugitive, I tried to channel my inner 'intrepid explorer'. But it was difficult to get excited when you felt guilty for abandoning a prisoner trapped in their own mind. I had asked if Mum wanted to join me, but she'd reluctantly declined, as if she wasn't ever allowed to lose her inhibitions and have fun. So I sallied forth, a tunnel of arched oaks inviting me to the adventures beyond.

Dad would have been in his element. For his sake I resolved to take in every precious brushstroke of nature's exhibition as I wound my way down the enticing sunken track. The root-veined sun-kissed pathway reached far down into the heart of the dene. It was protected by a sleeve of lichen-mottled beech trees and insulated by a luxuriant harlequin lining of flora. Lilac pincushions of scabious, rhubarb-and-custard-flecked bird's-foot-trefoil and coral clusters of red campion dazzled my rusty vision.

The further I ambled, the deeper I immersed myself in the baptismal water of the Washwell. Cyan flitters of an Adonis blue butterfly here, the gloating warble of an exhibitionist song thrush there; each threaded into this vivid tapestry.

Presently, I came upon an impenetrable-looking gate etched in maroon with a prominent 'BF'. Tethered in an unfathomable knot of cumbersome chains and armoured in moss through disuse, it was as if somebody didn't want their defences breached. The tumbledown excuse for a fingerpost definitely indicated it as a footpath, even if the yellow arrow had been weathered beyond all recognition. So I clambered over the battlements, eager to discover this forbidden kingdom.

Jumping down on the other side, I instantly understood why someone might want to possessively preserve this idyll. Opening up before me was our view from Heartsease magnified and embellished. A patchwork quilt of vast hills, small fields and little copses; embroidered with a labyrinth of broad hedgerows and trimmed with swathes of dense woodland.

Consulting my map, the footpath headed downhill towards the ribbon of the River Washwell, which plaited its way through the valley bottom. Aiming for the frill of woods running along the meadow's seam, my eyes and ears were captivated with yet more exquisite decorations to the vista. Spots of vermilion tissue-paper poppies susurrating in the breeze, the musical flourish of a tenacious chaffinch, all gilded with the glimpse of five fallow deer and a fawn at the forest edge.

Next time I would bring Dad's cherished binoculars with me. They'd also come in handy investigating the intriguing monstrosity of a mansion emerging through the trees.

Reaching a ramshackle stile, I paused to catch my breath. The air was uncomfortably close and it was unclear whether it was mizzle or beads of sweat that were moistening my brow. Scrambling over it, I trekked down the path which stitched its way through the ravine to the moonstone shimmer of the Washwell below.

The beech wood was a tangled warp and weft of kaleidoscope greens and gnarly umbers. It felt ancient yet teeming with life. A goldcrest's piercing falsetto, the pearl and turquoise flash of a jay and tuffets of raspberry-rippled orchids were all characters in this live drama. Undeterred by the plashing patters now pelting my T-shirt, I drenched myself in the delightful calm.

At length I came to the mother-of-pearl burble of the bustling brook. Now falling more heavily, the raindrops dinted and dimpled the rushing rill. Without waterproofs, I knew with a heavy heart that I would have to turn back. Maybe tomorrow I would reach Dad's tree, although I'd brace myself for a steep climb.

Pausing on the wooden footbridge, now slicked with puddles, my eyes were drawn to a toy sailing boat scudding along in the nacre froth. I suddenly felt my black and white drawbridge being pulled up. With tears scalding my eyes, I was back on the *Silver Myth* with Dad on our Norfolk Broads boating holiday. The rivulets of freshness coursing down my sodden jeans reminded me of the beads of condensation dripping from the windows of our quaint vessel. And if only the apology for a shower had gushed like this deluge! Although quirky, Dad's idea made sense after our encounter with a booming bittern one dusk, not to mention all of the other mesmerising forays into nature we had shared. Mum had said it wasn't her kind of thing and had gone on a spa break with Granny.

At this, my saturated body immediately bristled with barbs of panic and guilt. Why had I been so selfish? I'd left her all afternoon by herself with nobody to challenge her mental greyhound. Oh, how I hated the manipulative controlled stray that had replaced my Mum! Despite being a Daddy's girl, I cared about her enormously and so needed her to come back to me. I really missed our trips to the National Gallery and the strolls around St. James' Park with ice cream afterwards; I yenned to be eating apple strudel at the summit of the Zugspitze together, Mum all fired up recounting her childhood travels.

The drumming downpour cruelly echoed the ominous tattoo of Mum measuring out a precise quantity of pasta she wouldn't eat. How could I help her? If she would just let me in! Brimming over with regret, I bolted up the footpath, squalls of driving rain lashing against my trembling, worthless body.

The cloudburst was a fretful sea whipping up a frenzy. Waves of wild bluster crashed against listing trunks. Torrents of foam cascaded down the hillside, spattering everything in their wake with a muddied spray. The deafening scream of the jay was the ripping of a yacht's sails in the raging tempest, all of my fond boating memories torn to shreds with it. An avalanche of sludge hurtled from the approaching stile. Succumbing to the rollicking swell, I stumbled into a tangle of grimy brambles. No matter, I was already wet through; maybe it was punishment for my neglect of Mum?

Breathless from the treacherous ascent, I rested briefly at the stile and pulled out the soggy OS map from my back pocket. Finding my bearings, it reliably informed me that the imposing hall was Socknersh Manor, and that this was Giffords Wood. If I ever recovered from this baptism of fire, then perhaps Mum and I could soak up the charms of the landscape together. I pledged then and there to try and revitalise her. Our goal would be Trolliloes Forest and Dad's tree. As my mire-marinated curls dripped over the contours of promise, I braced myself for the offensive.

Fashioning the map into a makeshift umbrella, I hotfooted it across the claggy field. The whipped white mountain range-sky of the descent was now leaden with galloping grey horses whinnying in the struggle. I felt like a marabou stork wading through a Serengeti swamp, only less well equipped. It reminded me of that Scottish glen where Mum had got stuck in the mud and Dad had needed to rescue her. We were still chortling on return to our cosy loch-side bothy.

My parents had been like tailor-made bookends, perfectly complementing each other through the wear and tear of life. That is, until Dad's work had got in the way. Capstone Consulting had a lot to answer for. 'Building brighter futures' was their irritating slogan. If Dad had spent less time striving to 'eat the whole elephant', as the management consultants were wont to say, then maybe he wouldn't have had the heart attack. But even through his attempts to 'boil the ocean' Dad had doted on his 'little skylark', gently guiding Mum through her anxious flutters. I wished more than anything that she could soar and sing once more, Dad admiring her from above.

A monochrome mournful mist clouded my vision as I trudged through the endless quagmire. But now I was immune to the relentless volley of lashing rain. At brutal rock bottom, maybe I would see a panacea materialising through the melancholy murk?

I finally made it to the gate, the taunting clamour of an angry mob of crows as my accompaniment. Grappling with the boggy incline, it was as if I'd taken a different path to earlier. The jewels of the descent had been supplanted by a barbed jungle of fleshy totem pole-thistles, spiteful tongues of spiny holly and venomous violet vipers of creeping bittersweet.

My goose-pimpled skin crawled at the forlorn lowing of cattle. Ever since Dad and I were forced to dive-bomb over a hedge to escape a rabble of skittish cows, I'd developed a slight bovine phobia. Even lionhearted Dad had been a touch warier thereafter, tiptoeing through any livestock fields we'd encountered on our expeditions.

He was a big softie at heart. He blubbed his way through the *Up* DVD and had to hold back tears when he read *The Railway Children* as my bedtime story. What I would give for a bear hug with my daddy now, just like Bobbie got to! He would instantly cheer me up and tell me my sogginess was the badge of a true explorer. But Mum needed looking after more than I did right now. I desperately tried to quicken my footslog through the clag, even though it felt like I was wearing a poorly sealed diving suit that had let in half the North Sea. In fact, my afternoon yomp smacked of my toils as Mum's protector. A lot of effort for not much progress.

Surfacing from my slog, I felt as dejected as the doleful-eyed horses in the marshy field alongside me. The relief set in nonetheless as our gate appeared between the dribbling trees. Steeling myself for the home straight, I scuttled through the hammering flurries to Heartsease.

I was even gladder to see my green beacon of hope than when I'd returned home from the year 6 residential at Llanfestgog. Although I was probably just as wet and cold – Olivia Mason had even caught hypothermia on our gorge scramble! Thank goodness the car was in the shingle shore-driveway and the lamps were on in the lighthouse. Mum would be safe.

I hastened through the gritty quicksand, keen to hold her close. She was doubtless fretting about me and would want to reciprocate. As if she, quite literally, didn't have enough on her plate. How could I have been so unthinking? I vowed to be less egocentric. If I could help her to fly as Dad had done so selflessly, then perhaps my infernal magpie would take wing too.

Finding the back door unlocked, I instantly relaxed. Everything was going to be just fine. Certainly when I'd dried off it would. Maybe I'd make a hot chocolate to share together once I'd showered? I needed to crack down on the greyhound more, to silence its howling excuses. I feigned positivity to break the ice:

'Well, that was interesting! Not quite what I'd hoped for! Still, the valley's stunning, Mum, and I really want to share it with you. You'll love it!'

I was met with a disconcerting silence.

I darted down the corridor, scanning each room and leaving a trail of drips behind me. She was probably on the toilet, or perhaps even making a start on dinner if she was feeling brave. I really craved those fancy sausages she'd dared to buy. What could be more comforting than a plate of sausages and mash with gravy? It had been Dad's desert island meal. Or could she have had a challenging afternoon, gone into her shell and be doing that exasperating thing where she blanked me. I honestly wouldn't mind if I caught her doing burpees to her '90s club classics CD; I was just dying to see her.

Fizzing with excitement in anticipation of that cuddle, I veered around the corner into the open-plan living space. I scoured the room for her spindly frame, my heart pummelling my chest mercilessly. My drained limbs stiffened with each agonising pace. Reaching the vile monochrome rug, I dissolved into a piebald puddle of despair. Mum was nowhere to be found.

# THREE FOR A GIRL

B loodthirsty baying froze me to the spot in the fern-freckled woodland clearing. Pricking up my ears to scope out the impending peril, my twitching whiskers bristled at the hurtling cacophony. We were far from the warren with no hole to flee down. Alerting the other does, I thumped my hind feet fiercely in the soil and raised my trembling tail. With bulging eyes, we sprang and scampered through the Lincolnshire fenland in a stampede of fright. I was now separated from the rest of the colony, the gnashing greyhound hot on my heels as it bounded over the furrowed earth. Skimming creeks and scooting through hedges, frisking over ditches and bolting into copses. All was in vain in this fated barbaric pursuit. Leaping from a snarl of nettles, the savage beast pounced upon my wired, palpitating body…

My reverie was mercifully interrupted by the car-swerving squawk of a daft pheasant. Spooked by the racket, the rabbit that had prompted my musing scuttered off over the footbridge. I was keen to exorcise the distressing memories of yesterday and followed its lead out into the soughing cornfield. And what a difference a day made! Yesterday I'd been imprisoned in a toxic snow globe, a violent monsoon eddying around in my brimming brain. Today I was part of a nurturing terrarium of solace, ripples of ultramarine lustre illuminating me from within. Regrettably, I was still flanked by the magpie and the greyhound.

I meandered along the field-edge path, rivulets of glisten floodlit from the dappled beech parasol overhead. I felt increasingly pessimistic about my ability to help Mum. She'd breezed in at nine o'clock last night, utterly oblivious to the panic she'd induced. Wringing wet and shivering uncontrollably, she'd spent most of the evening welded to the radiator in an attempt to thaw her fragile frame. Always a glutton for punishment, she'd rounded off proceedings with a thrashing of abdominal crunches and half a vegetable cup-a-soup as her measly recompense.

I'd bent over backwards desperately striving to get through to her. I'd ensured I didn't give her a disparaging lecture. I'd even offered to cook whatever she fancied for dinner and suggested we watch the next episode of *Gilmore Girls* to unwind. Instead, I was subjected to an evening of silence with a frantic automaton. It was challenging loving the waif that had ousted my mum. Yes, this was an aggravated form of torture, just like my rabbit-coursing daydream.

Before long I encountered a smart-looking gate emblazoned with a maroon 'BF'. Tacked in the centre was an arresting flyer which read:

*Socknersh Game and Country Fair*
*Monday 26th August 2019 9am–5pm*
*Relish a day in the countryside with your loved ones!*
*Our peerless pageant presents a cornucopia of*
*pastoral pleasures for your delectation:*

*• Shooting, game and fishing competitions • Gundog scurries*
*• Falconry displays • Countryside demonstrations, fine arts and rural crafts*
*• Grand floral pavilion • Ferret racing • Hog roast and beer tent*
*• Shopping opportunities – rifles, country clothing,*
*gun accessories and game food*

*Tickets on the door – Adults £18, Children £10, Dogs welcome*

Ever since my research for the debating society on illegal coursing, any blood sport had repulsed me – the thought of innocent sentient creatures mutilated for someone's amusement. And even if I'd wanted to go, I didn't have anybody to accompany me. My morose magpie hovered above as I imagined merry throngs of carefree families having fun together – the resounding cheers at the dog agility course, the huddles of grinning, grubby kids savouring ice creams as big as their heads and the astounded gasps for the man whittling a grizzly bear with a chainsaw. I felt like the fifty-two-hertz whale, drifting aimlessly through an ocean of loneliness where nobody could hear my feeble, despairing calls for help.

Besides, who could I talk to? Granny was always more intent on regaling me with tales of her friends at the tennis club and kept on commenting on how 'trim' Mum was looking. Auntie Ruth always seemed to be burning the candle at both ends baking scones for her tearoom. And Caitlin was spending a fortnight at a Tuscan villa with her family. Anyway, she'd been keeping me at arm's length since Dad had died and Mum's behaviour had deteriorated. It hadn't helped that Mum had turned up late to prize-giving and had spent the evening hell-bent on denying herself a slice of celebratory cake. There'd definitely been some hushed tittle-tattle in the corridors as we'd left.

I needed Mum to thrive before September. That would avoid the embarrassment of being the girl who had to childmind her 'peculiar, sickly' mother. It would be useful to start afresh with friends at my new school. I cursed myself for this spasm of selfishness. If only people could be bothered to fathom the 'real' Mum! In a moment of déjà vu, my heaving head was swamped with a flash flood of anguish. Should I march her to the doctors myself? Was there a helpline I should be contacting? But escapism didn't have to signify defeatism. I was determined to draw on my wild wanderings to find a way forward.

I forged along the sunbathed footpath towards the formidable mansion looming at the far corner of the field. The pasture was a chessboard of giant Shredded Wheat hay bales and was swaddled in a blanket of wildflower garlands. My eyes were bedazzled by a bloom of indigo rampion 'jellyfish' billowing in the breeze. I savoured the golden dandelion brooches clasped on green-cardiganed breasts and the filigree tussocks of ivory meadowsweet. If Mum would just risk blossoming as they did, instead of remaining in her tight, 'safe' bud!

The explosive firework display cry of a jackdaw was a fitting fanfare to my arrival at the manor house. Straddling the stile, I assimilated each hideous detail of this lavish pile. As I edged goggle-eyed across the lane, it summoned up visions of the palace at Versailles on last summer's French road trip. Awestruck by its vastness, I loitered open-mouthed at the towering wrought-iron gates.

These gilded Curly Wurly bars were forged into a giant protruding 'BF' and were policed by a pair of odious black-and-white marble corvids. Beyond them lay a formal parterre crammed with clashing fluorescent bedding and distasteful topiary alligators that seemed to be limbering up for a dip in the immense central fountain. Greek mythology had never been my strong point at school, but the epic bronze statue at the centre could well have been Narcissus judging by the grandiosity of this pleasure palace. Encircling him spurted seven gargantuan chameleon jets as high as the turreted roof. The château itself was hewn out of harsh gunmetal granite and was guarded at its east and west wings by ornate twin corkscrew towers. The dour façade was accessorised with gaudy elaborate balconies and loathsome limestone busts which looked out bemusedly over the palm-adorned terrace. Crowning the hall's ostentation was a gleaming belvedere cupola at its nucleus. My eyes ached from their workout in pretentiousness. The ramble up to Trolliloes Forest would be their cooldown.

Returning readily to the footpath, the wider estate opened up beyond the gold-lacquered railings to my left. There was an enormous boating lake complete with duck island and kitsch grotto, a roaming herd of piebald alpacas and a preposterous trelliswork aviary. The owner clearly had more money than sense. I retreated to the cool, shaded avenue of sweet chestnut-candelabra, the feathery pale blossom-candles providing a softer illumination for my onward journey.

I tarried in the stippled sunlight to admire the blushing spires of foxgloves that were also delighting in the sanctuary. This was certainly the social hub for Sussex's pheasant population! The befuddled birds zig-zagged along the path like drunk drivers, careering hither and thither to no purpose. Incapable of appreciating the serenity, these extroverts of the valley spluttered and sputtered haphazardly to and fro.

The bewildered bouquet drew my eyes to a burly silhouette gesticulating crazily at a cowering figure. The intimidator obviously had a flea in his ear about something. Jumping into his gleaming ebony four-by-four with a hefty door slam, he sped off towards me with a squeal of tyres. With pheasants flailing rowdily in all directions, I was forced to duck into the verge to avoid being hit. Wedged up against a fetid straggle of mugwort, I gave the irate driver a long hard stare and was dumbfounded by the incandescent eyes glaring back at me.

Surely it couldn't be? I hurriedly scrutinised his glower as he zoomed by. Mouth agape with incredulity, I watched the owner of vehicle number plate 'BELL 1' swerve towards Socknersh. It was unmistakably him, without a shadow of doubt. The oppressive fuming 'Lord of the Manor' was my dad's chief antagonist! I'd just nearly been run over by CEO of Capstone Consulting and all-round moron, Hugo Bellington-Fraser.

If people talked of cats that got the cream, then Hugo Bellington-Fraser was the king of the pride that devoured the whole dazzle of zebras. Or at least commanded the rest of his troop to hunt it for him. His smug face had lamentably been the default screensaver on Dad's company laptop and I'd grown to loathe his compassionless eyes. With his polished crocodile-leather winklepickers, brylcreemed raven hair and matching houndstooth silk cravat and waistcoat, he had a ripe scent of narcissism about him. Dad always joshed that you could smell Hugo's questionable aftershave long before he clamped eyes on you. Just like his odour, there was an awful lot of wafting and drifting with this ravenous fat-cat. Indeed, he was perfectly willing for his devoted pride to fight off the alligators so that he could paddle out the swamp.

Ascending past the scene of the earlier altercation, I hoped that the cringing inhabitant of grimly titled 'Beggar's Well' didn't feel as abused as the employees of Capstone Consulting. The poky tumbledown lodge with its tiny leaded-light windows and primitive appearance stirred up the dungeon of Dad's mind shortly before he died.

Diligent and eager to please, he had not only 'picked the low-hanging fruit' from the tree but had lovingly harvested the whole orchard for the rest of the staff to feast on. He'd demonstrated each of the corporation's 'first-rate foundational pillar stones' (Drive, Ownership, Leadership and the absurdly dubbed Titanic Spirit). Yet his Herculean struggles meant he hadn't sorted out his own lifejacket. Whilst he was in steerage enduring fruitless 'ideation sessions', Hugo had been airlifted to his private castillo in the Caribbean. As the tension had ramped up, so had Dad's blood pressure. And Mum and I had watched powerlessly as our prop slipped away. Torpid, distant and pessimistic absolutely wasn't our first-class dad. The nadir had irrefutably been reached when he'd stowed away in the toilets at the famed quarterly meet-up to evade 'going under'.

If only aspiring ecologist Dad had been blessed with the self-compassion to retrain as a countryside ranger. And now his tormentor was effectively our next-door neighbour! I would refrain from blurting this out to Mum, dreading a dramatic spiralling of her intolerable shenanigans. Dad had often chuntered about Hugo's footling corporate jargon. 'Let's shave that poodle!' had been his inanity of choice. I hankered for vengeance – to shear this heinous hound and lay bare his true inept hideousness.

Embittered and with my saturnine magpie thrashing around in my head, I returned to nature. Yet even the thin, sorrowful strain of a robin echoed my sombre mood. The lane had now tapered to a rutted bridleway hedged with berry-bespeckled hawthorn. It threaded its way up past scrambles of downy old man's beard, resplendent trumpets of fragrant honeysuckle and the joyful, flushed faces of a clambering dog rose.

By and by I came to a stile, the jaunty maraca-jiggling of a grasshopper as my backing. I swivelled round to take in the view under the carmine-dotted cocoon of a rowan tree. Beneath me spread out a living quilt of green and blue tartan, just like the one Mum and Dad had at Durrington Gardens. My eyes tracked my undulating journey from the foliate pillow of Heartsease, through bobbled thickets and crinkled fields, past the greasy stain of Socknersh and up to where my feet now snuggled. The panorama would only be enhanced as I neared the summit.

Scrabbling over into the pasture beyond, bubbles of excitement fizzed through me as I realised the proximity of my holy grail. One more grassy trek and I would conquer the crest and enter Trolliloes Forest. Dad's tree was even discernible at the very apex!

I stepped up the tempo in anticipation, racing cumulus ice skaters as my pacemaker. Huddled amongst the spinney to my far right was a homely farmstead and on my left towards the brow of the hill stood a tasteless neoclassical folly. I assumed this showy mini Arc de Triomphe was another of Hugo's egotistical indulgences. I so hoped the local bird population had appropriated it as a handy public convenience.

Fatigued by my strenuous ascent, the rippling grassland ocean attempted to swallow me up in its swishing surf. Patrolling the coastline, a circling buzzard egged me on to the kissing gate which beckoned me into Trolliloes.

Closing it behind me, I instantly felt protected by the verdant gingham cloak which enveloped me. Shimmering solitaires of sunlight twirled on the track and coaxed me further under the wadded beech thatch. A blue tit enticed me deeper as it bounced ahead with the lightness and agility of a rainbow-marbled rubber ball. Another hundred metres and I'd arrive at the colossal spreading tree!

Drifts of fuchsia cyclamen hearts lined the home stretch. I skipped towards its bronzed torso, eager to wrap my arms around it. Its muscular branches waved me underneath its tousled emerald mop. I nuzzled up against its brindled bark and imbibed its mellow, earthy smell. The beech tree *was* Dad. With its clean-shaven skin and its uncanny facility for encouragement, it heartened my subjugated mind. Still clinging to its smooth middle, I marvelled at the lush sapphire-encrusted frill of forget-me-nots which skirted its trunk. An uninhibited sobbing fit followed, a gazing prismatic peacock butterfly my only onlooker.

Weeping against its consoling body, a faint whirring began to trickle through my ears. This dialled up to a melodious bombination and amplified to a fervent sputtering. With an instant spring in my step, I felt the urge to caper around this living maypole. Blaring crackles now coursed through my ear canals, as if I was tuning in to a different radio frequency. My head throbbed at the novel tumult and I clutched my comfort blanket more tightly. Had I developed tinnitus? Could I be having a stroke? Or was my tyrannised brain finally exploding?

My blood had suddenly become effervescent, frothy tingles flooding through my veins. A raging wanderlust welled up inside of me and I ventured out into the uncharted jungle, a gentle murmur still resounding in my ears. I would be an intrepid explorer, for old time's sake.

With each sublime step along the snaking variegated track, my burdensome brain was chain by chain unshackled. I was as much a part of this animate jigsaw as the lime-fronded carpet of ferns or the feverish squirrels frolicking amongst it. Tears of rapture were now prickling my eyelids.

Unexpectedly, a muted, snuffly voice rose out of the incessant thrumming: 'Are you alright, miss?'

I was startled by this abrupt interruption, assuming that I had this sylvan paradise to myself. Maybe I'd dropped my map and a kindly rambler wanted to hand it back? Or perhaps a seething farmer was about to admonish me for trespassing? Swinging round, I was quite stunned by the unbelievable sight which met my astounded eyes. For there, in the middle of the pathway, sat a smiling, gingery, bright-eyed bunny.

## Chapter 4

# Four for a boy

'Would you like to share my clover cuddly? It always makes me feel better,' enquired the soft, eager voice, proffering the treasured stem of clover it had been nuzzling.

Pinching myself at the fact that an auburn, chocolate button-eyed rabbit was conversing with me, I felt moved at its empathetic gesture. This potential figment of my imagination was more in touch with my emotions than anyone else had cared to be since Dad's death.

Threshing about in my tangled mind in its disrespectful rakish tuxedo, my vexatious magpie had boycotted my mourning at every turn. Could this be a hallucination of heartache, an indication that my arch-enemy was slackening its stranglehold? In religious studies I remembered learning about the Jewish tradition of covering mirrors following a bereavement. With its penchant for shiny objects, maybe my kleptomaniac foe had pilfered my ability to let any true peek of Dad, or indeed myself, into my lacklustre life. That is, until now. Perhaps this vision of grief was my battered brain retreating to bittersweet memories of my naturalist hero? My world had become so colourless that even reality was no match for my yearning. What was the harm in rolling with this far-fetched fantasy? Who knows, this blethering bronze bunny might help me puzzle out my perplexing Rubik's Cube-head.

Gambolling towards us at top speed came another juvenile leporine friend brandishing a string of well-nibbled dandelions. 'You can borrow my blowball blanket if you like,' piped the hazel, fawn-eyed companion.

Dumbstruck by this probable delusion, it felt like I was caught up in a tangible *Aesop's Fable*.

'When my whiskers are droopy, I like to go joggletailing in the kingcups,' peeped the original elfin enthusiast.

'And if my tail is fringling, prickleballing down the stallionback is a good distraction!' shrieked the second excitedly.

I would evidently need to master a whole novel lexicon to understand these two genial tots.

'And don't forget chasing flitterblossoms! Or doing some bobgazing!' squealed the coppery little one.

Watching them jiggling around in elation at the prospect of a new playmate, it was only fair to break my impertinent silence: 'I'm okay, thanks; actually I think I'm glad instead of sad. You're lucky to live in such charming woodland.'

How did one make conversation with a couple of fidgety, warm-hearted bunnies? I'd go with the freakish flow, treating them like my spirited toddling cousin Alfie.

'So what are your names then?' I asked courteously. 'My name's Ella.'

Bobbing around boisterously like he had ticks in his fur, the elder one chimed in keenly: 'I'm Wilbur and this is my little brother Wilf. I'm two months and six days old and Mummy says I can have a special prittleleaping party for my birthjamboree. We live in elderberry warren near the crooked yew. And I think your name is pretty.'

I was thankful for this fervent verbosity; it wasn't every day that one had the opportunity to shoot the breeze with a prattling bunny. Spellbound, I laboriously calculated that Wilbur was six given a wild rabbit's life expectancy was about three years. Oh, to be six again and deaf to the babel of life! Hitting double figures seemed to denote an inhibition growth spurt.

'What's prittleleaping?' I ventured, still incredulous that I was rabbiting on with, errr… a rabbit.

'Just because I'm the kit, doesn't mean I can't stand on my own four paws,' blubbered Wilf disgruntledly, his bottom lip trembling.

'Oh, don't get your tail in a tangle, Wilfy!' taunted a smirking Wilbur.

A diversion was always a good tactic with kids; hopefully it would prove equally fruitful with a couple of quarrelling bunnies. Anxious to avoid conflict, I decided to intervene in the tiff: 'How about you boys show me some of these wonderful games you've been talking about? I'm raring to go if you are?'

'Oooo, yes, can we, can we, Miss Ella?' cheeped an instantly enlivened Wilf.

'I'm full of grass and hot to hop! To the stallionback!' whooped an electrified Wilbur.

After much exhilarated jigging and jumping, the boys animatedly ushered me back along the smiling shimmer-stippled track. Springing hither and thither as if on pogo sticks, it was difficult for me to keep up with these ebullient rascals. The sheltered woodland floor was strewn with feathery moss-cushions and provided an excellent hopscotch course. Frisking about delightedly under the diaphanous beech vault, they were reviving my optimism with each blissful bob.

'Wow, check out this whopper, Miss Ella!' hollered a triumphant Wilbur, waggling a stick as large as a Flemish giant rabbit in my direction.

What was it with boys and sticks? Even Dad had fashioned fallen branches into improvised shepherd's crooks on our wild escapades.

'Just feast your eyes on mine!' warbled a proud Wilf, flourishing a prize-winning carrot-sized twig.

'Woah, a flitterblossom, a flitterblossom! I bet I can run at sixty million hindleaps an hour and catch it! Just you watch, Ella!' speculated a restless Wilbur, capering after a tangerine-speckled butterfly with his giggling brother hot on his hocks.

Where did they get all their energy from? I felt frazzled just observing them cavort along the amethyst-studded pathway. Weaving to and fro amongst the twinkling columbine dunes, now seemingly on space hoppers, their euphoric squeals filled the heady air. They pranced towards the rusted kissing gate like mad March hares, secreting themselves behind a bloom-gilded spiny gorse. I entertained their cheeky hide-and-seek prank even though I could increasingly identify with a beached whale:

'Wilbur! Wilf! I wonder where those impish scamps could be?'

'Boo!' they screeched simultaneously, peeping out from the glimmering bush with beaming faces.

'Bet you didn't guess we were here! Now let's prittleleap!' cried Wilbur rambunctiously.

It was as if this hyperactive pair had ambushed the Easter Bunny and nibbled through all of his chocolate. Their sheer unbounded energy truly invigorated my flummoxed, fatigued mind. Prittleleaping appeared to be a form of cunicular trampolining. Clinging to the gate's scabrous crosspieces with their front paws, they flung their muscular hind limbs skyward Buckaroo-style. Peals of laughter reverberated around the verdant cathedral.

I perused the visual nature encyclopaedia which opened up beyond, although currently it felt more like I was caught up in a fanciful fairytale. Rambling rabbits, pretentious palaces and vile villains had characterised my page-turner of a day.

'Behold the stallionback!' bawled a gesturing Wilf, eager to galvanise me into action pronto.

The stallionback was clearly their nickname for the hill which sloped away gently like the rugged topline of an Appaloosa horse. They squeezed effortlessly through a chink in the barbed-wire fence and motioned exuberantly for me to follow suit. Whilst I did seem to be stuck in a bizarre sort of Wonderland, I presumed that my superpower wouldn't stretch to Alice's famous shrinking feat. As I jostled with the rickety gate, the zesty tykes performed their version of *Riverdance* in anticipation.

'To joggletail?' quizzed a vivacious Wilbur.

'Or to prickleball?' probed Wilf, looking like a rabbit with two scuts.

Now I seemed to have entered a surreal leporine game show. Thus far, I'd hit the joyous jackpot with everything these handsome assistants had so dynamically thrown at me.

'Let's joggletail! That sounds wonderful!' I proposed, keen to enter into the spirit.

With whoops of glee, they bounded off helter-skelter to the bottom of the field. Spread along its sun-baked heel was a generous slather of creamy buttercups, ideal for a game of hide-and-seek. I rejoiced as they romped around, their tails jouncing wildly like a cheerleader's pompoms. How they then found the stamina to scoot off pell-mell to the summit I do not know!

'Come on, Ella! Don't drag your paws!' called an indefatigable Wilbur.

'Please can you prickleball with us, Miss Ella? Pretty please!' begged a hopeful, winsome Wilf.

Catching my breath at the balmy brow, I chuckled as they rolled up into balls and hurled themselves down the pockmarked hill. It brought back fond memories of our annual Dartmoor jaunts, Dad and I launching ourselves similarly down some obscure tor, our hearty laughter infusing the summery Devon air. These scallywags' enthusiasm was infectious and I itched to break free from my cramped black-and-white hutch.

'To hell with it! Why not?' I yelled, hatching out of my incarcerating piebald shell.

Connecting with the springy turf beneath me felt like a reunion with a long-lost friend. I relished every blissful bump of the undulating descent.

'Woohoo, go Ella!' cheered the cheeky duo in unison, dancing an expressive celebratory bhangra.

'It's so fun, isn't it!' trilled an excitable Wilf, wiggling around like a captivating cunicular marionette.

'It makes my head spin like a sycamore whirligig!' agreed a buoyed-up Wilbur.

As we clambered once again up the ridge, Wilbur suggested a round of bobgazing, which sounded like cloud watching from the gabbled explanation. Maybe they'd finally been tired out? Wilf certainly looked as if he was beginning to peter out. We flopped our weary bodies down on a trio of comfy-looking lichen-velveted stumps near the forest edge. A gentle zephyr provided refreshing air-conditioning. The bunnies reinvigorated with their chickweed and mallow pick 'n' mix, our cumulus screening commenced.

'Me first! Me first!' clamoured an impatient Wilbur. 'You see that one there?' he said, pointing at a drifting wisp of cirrus. 'That reminds me of the nasty monster with bramble-thorn teeth which made Mummy's fur curl last week. He was horrible! He had eyes that bulged like ripe gooseberries and paws as big as Daddy with ginormous talons on! He didn't even have any fur, just black-and-white patches over his scrawny skeleton! And there was a beastly stinky man with greasy black hair clapping too! Mummy hasn't come out of our burrow since that frightful hullabaloo!' he graphically gushed, self-satisfied at his nightmarish description.

'I keep having bad dreams about terrible ogres with growls as scary as the farmer's grass-gobbling giant!' spurted a quaking, wide-eyed Wilf.

From the gibbered narrative, I surmised that this macabre monstrosity was a dog. Could I even dare to presume that the sinister scoundrel was Hugo? Rabbit coursing sounded just like his kind of hollow horseplay.

The terror-struck twosome both began to whimper. Wilf snuggled tightly to his clover comforter. I felt their pain; my mum too was trapped in a warren of paralysing restrictions, tormented by a heinous hellhound. Right now I'd rather be au pair to these dear delights than have to nanny my ailing mother. My insides were in a pied flutter contemplating the homecoming to my poor, doe-eyed waif. But these little gems were wilting and I would need to leave soon.

'That all sounds petrifying! I do hope your mum's okay?' I enquired, yearning fruitlessly that somebody would ask me the same question.

'I-I-I don't want to talk about the fur-raising bogeybuck anymore,' wailed a worried Wilbur.

'Waaaaaah, waaaaaah,' snivelled Wilf, shaking like a dandelion leaf.

Stroking each between the ears, I desperately tried to change the subject: 'It must be my turn now. I wonder what I'll see?'

Whatever I chose, it had to be positive. I couldn't leave these eternal optimists on a sad note.

'This one here, you see that?' I remarked, motioning at a mountainous mound of cumulonimbus. 'That conjures up the South Downs for me,' I suggested, smiling at the carefree wildlife expeditions this evoked.

'What is the sowthdownz?' queried a pepped-up Wilbur.

Wilf looked like his eyes were glazing over. I needed to keep this brief.

'It's a herd of stallions balancing on top of each other. Just think of the megaprickleballing you could do!' I explained, Wilbur's eyes lighting up at this tantalising prospect.

'It makes me think of my dad and all the amazing adventures we had there together. Once my hat was whipped off by the wind and we had to dart off after it! It landed up in a disused chalk pit where we admired the twinkling blue flitterblossoms and spotted deer. Or the time we got lost in the dark and glistening glow worms steered us back to safety,' I recalled, attempting to hold back tears.

'Wow! That sounds brilliant! I wish you could take us there, Ella. What's your dad's name and how old is he and what's his favourite colour?' badgered an inquisitive Wilbur. Wilf was now curled up in a daisy divan, gently snoring.

'My dad's dead,' I replied, now mewling and tugging at my curls in grievance.

The funeral knell tolled harshly. Its emphatic clang jarred my pained ears. How could I ever explain the complicated jiggle-joggle of emotions I was experiencing to two flagging bunnies?

'Oh, I'm sorry, Miss Ella,' Wilbur commiserated, holding out a dock leaf tissue he'd picked.

'That happened to Uncle Kelvin last week. He caught strangleeye lurgy down near the wormpuddle. Then there's second cousin Felicity who was snatched by an orange bushy-tailed savage four days ago. And yesterday our little sister Josephine was squished by a toppling oak tree. But you can still have all those adventures, Ella. They'll just be with new friends.'

These juvenile joys were a perfect lesson in transience. In a rabbit's world, death was always lurking around the corner, whether from disease, predator or misadventure. When you were lucky to survive your first year, every precious second counted. So why not choose to prickleball, instead of wallowing in a drooping, fringly, magpie-shaped mound?

'Well, I think I'd better be off,' I announced reluctantly.

Dad's heart attack had been so sudden that I hadn't had the chance to say goodbye properly. I wanted to ensure that there was a fitting farewell this time. Who knows, would I see, or indeed communicate with these sweethearts ever again? But it was definitely time to depart. Wilf was out for the count and even irrepressible Wilbur was nodding off. Besides, I didn't want to be accused of kitnapping by an irked daddy buck.

'Oh, do you have to! Please can you stay for tea? Daddy's making a comforting clover casserole,' implored a subdued Wilbur.

It was tempting given my prospective evening. I was in a black-and-white flap just envisaging another distressing dinner with its elaborate excuses, all topped off with a goodnight squabble.

'There's nothing I'd like more than to stay. But I'm afraid my mummy needs me home,' I glumly admitted.

'Please, please can you come back tomorrow? We could go blackberrying and give you the guided tour of the warren,' pleaded an equally downcast Wilbur.

'Let's see what tomorrow brings, hey? It's been a pleasure meeting you both. And I've so enjoyed our fun. Thank you so much, you've helped me more than you'll ever know,' I maundered, hoping that partings wouldn't always be this challenging.

I mooched morosely down the field, turning every so often to wave and grin at the now-perky pair. They'd floodlit my pitch-black brain like fluorescent disco lights. My cherished dock leaf souvenir would be a reminder that even happy bunnies sometimes needed to cry.

The yattering youths had vanished by the time I reached the ivy-wreathed stile. Had it all just been an absurd illusion? My ears still thrummed relentlessly and spicules of euphoria charged through my veins. Scrambling over, I paused to watch a leopard-print comma resting on a trumpet of honeysuckle and chortled at the thought of Wilbur and Wilf bounding after it.

As I touched down on the other side, the constant clangour subsided. My skin felt clammy and a frantic fluttering impulse to return to Mum took over. Was I now deafened to the vivace voices of the valley? I climbed hastily back over the stile, eager to tune in to the wavelength of the Washwell once more. But other than the 'tee-hee' sniggering of a derisive seagull, it was deadly quiet. Its mocking was justified; this had obviously been a cruel chimera. Just like old Mrs. Rabbit, I now had a real-life poorly bunny to put to bed. To my chagrin, a table-spoonful of camomile tea would not be the simple panacea.

At the foot of the stile, albino clusters of clover hedgehogs took me back to the comfort and joy of my droll daydream. I would strive to learn from the moral of the tale. A last desperate attempt to fine-tune my ears was in vain, the only interference being the 'kak-kak' of some bird up near Hugo's ludicrous victory arch. I couldn't procrastinate any longer. Just like Dad, I was a wanderer and the trek home would bolster me.

Mounting the stile for one last time, my eyes focused on a neat 'AP' inscribed on the timber. How serendipitous that Dad's initials were carved on the gateway to my jubilant imagined adventure. Perhaps another Andy Pearson had hiked through this meadow, or indeed Dad himself – his memory never had been that sharp. He'd nicknamed me his 'little ele', joking that I could probably recall the outfit he was wearing when I was born. Unfortunately, my elephantine ability to never forget was my problem right now.

Sadly my piebald pickpocket was back, flailing around in my face and nabbing the mirror to my soul. Consequently the journey back was a blurry zoetrope of flickering fuzziness. Cerise curlicues of red bartsia here, flashes of a chestnut and olive firecrest there, and snatched peeps of indifferent sheep wheezing in the warmth.

The human faces I encountered only ruffled my meddlesome magpie further. Passing Beggar's Well, I met the aggrieved eyes of a fellow Atlas, bearing the weight of the world on his shoulders. This morning's harrowed hunchback scuttled swiftly towards his monochrome prison, secreting himself from his nefarious nemesis. The scar of Socknersh disfigured my journey further. A glimpse of Hugo blasting clay pigeons like a poncey tweeded Mr. McGregor was enough to whip me up into a black-and-white frenzy.

At the footbridge, I appeared to have descended even further down the rabbit hole. *Strangleeye lurgy*, that's what they'd called it. I could see why as I pitied the pustulous glassy-eyed scrap hobbling along the riverbank beside me. Peppering the sultry air with stertorous rasps, this wretched shred of a rabbit undoubtedly had myxomatosis. Just like with my forlorn, fading mum, I wished that there was something I could do to salvage this sorry scrap. Had this insufferable plague been introduced deliberately by a peeved farmer, or even a splenetic Hugo? Hopefully it wouldn't reach Wilbur and Wilf. But of course, they probably didn't exist, and my mum, whilst in extremis, did. If only a straightforward vaccine was the cure for Mum's pernicious pestilence of the mind.

Famished from my cerebral fug, I needed sustenance for the gruelling climb ahead. A fridge dotted with diet yoghurts and groaning with greens was enough to put anybody off their food. Fumbling in my pocket for a toffee, I chanced upon a withering dock leaf. What use would this disquieting memento mori be?

In my bulky black-and-white cavalry uniform, I grappled with the steep ascent towards my Armageddon. The cobalt tie-dye sky was now a muddied mishmash of murk. Not unlike my oppressive busby-hatted head. The remainder of the slog was a salvo of fragmentary flickers. Violet bullets of spiky teasel assaulted me in the meadows. Over the gate, a bird's decomposing carcass was the cheerless casualty of a fox's cut-throat campaign. Nearing home, the tapping tattoo of a partridge was a pressing call to arms. Passing the still-dejected horses, I ached to shroud myself in the virescent brindled camouflage of the countryside.

As the Heartsease sign came into view, my heart began beating like a drummer boy's snare. Yesterday she'd been missing in action; what would be Mum's fate today?

Reaching the gate, I relaxed as I caught sight of Mum up near the French doors. Prostrated on the York stone patio and shackled by her repulsive gym kit, I assumed that she was subjecting herself to some sort of planking-punishment. But my bright-eyed and bushy-tailed gym bunny was unnervingly still.

As I sprinted hysterically up the driveway, my maleficent magpie began a barbaric dive-bombing attack. Swooping in front of my terrorised eyes like a murderous missile, it stabbed the back of my harrowed head with its belligerent beak. As I tore dementedly across the lawn, the gaping gash on Mum's gaunt forehead became glaringly obvious. Pummelling me with vindictive pecks, my monstrous magpie mobbed my flustered mind. This was my piebald penance for abandoning her.

My panic-stricken gaze raked guiltily over Mum's cadaverous, pallid body. Traumatised by her pitiful, hollow-eyed emaciation, perhaps I should let my nemesis finish me off? Yes, this would be my just deserts, my merciless death the ultimate corvine retribution for the unforgivable neglect.

CHAPTER 5

# FIVE FOR SILVER

Entombed amongst the odds and ends of the final packing box, I happened upon the silver filigree skylark. It was as though Mum had been attempting to bury the pain of Dad's passing whilst knowing that she'd eventually need to confront it.

The intricate necklace had been his typically thoughtful gift for their sixth wedding anniversary. Cradling its graceful glinting wings in my palm, I imagined it soaring into the striated sapphire skies. Hovering high above the yarrow-stippled downland, it launched into its ebollimento exaltation before parachuting deftly to its corn-curtained refuge. The charm's glimmering elegance had enhanced Mum's dainty features. It had been as much a part of her daily attire as the flamboyant silk scarves and trusty Breton tote bag. That is, until Dad's funeral, as if this final farewell signalled the rejection of any relic worship. I now wished that my discovery could be the silver lining to last week's charged thundercloud warning.

It had hopefully been the low-water mark of our drought-stricken reservoir. Mum had been ebbing away for months and I'd been relentlessly desiccated by despair watching her. Arid from anguish, both of us had been gasping for a sip of joy since the searing sorrow of Dad's death.

The terrifying moment I'd discovered her ashen, lifeless body would undoubtedly be scorched into my memory forever more. All of a sudden she'd thankfully come round, allowing my piebald petrification to ease somewhat. But within moments I was sadly reduced to a furious flapping magpie muddle at Mum's insistence that she didn't need an ambulance and that one more jogging circuit of the garden was necessary! Reeking of pear-drop ketones and staggering around like an exercise junkie, she blacked out again mid-lunge, forcing me to catch her.

I was reluctant to desert this wavering wisp of bewilderment but it was imperative to call 999 and somehow get some sugar down her. It was like Grandpa Arthur with his diabetic hypos, although I could guarantee that there wouldn't be any Mars bars hanging around in our cupboards.

Propping her up with the rolled-up garden furniture cover, I darted desperately for the back door. Plagued by painful piebald paraesthesia, I gibbered through the emergency call. I frantically scoured the bare larder for something calorific whilst subjected to a persistent pinto picana. Stashed at the very back of the highest cupboard, I managed to dredge up a small gluten-free loaf and a jar of strawberry conserve. I passed on butter knowing that she'd kick up a fuss about the added deliciousness and hurriedly daubed a couple of slices with the scarlet ambrosia.

Motoring back out to my iron-willed invalid, I was welted once more with waves of black-and-white hysteria. After protracted cajoling that additional press-ups weren't required, I sat her on the wall like a shattered Humpty Dumpty. Shuddering with starvation, she stubbornly refused to sample a scrap of scrumptiousness. Steely-eyed in its determination to deny even a crumb of self-indulgence, her unrelenting greyhound gripped her in a stranglehold.

After mind-numbing months of acquiescing to this heartless

hound, I appreciated that Mum had to *want* to set it free. It was all very well me coaxing her to stomach a smidgen, but unless *she* had an appetite for emancipation, recovery would elude us. If she was somehow trying to subject herself to the agony of Dad's heart attack, then I'm sure he was finding her self-flagellation far more excruciating. I certainly was.

The keening of a siren wafted down Flitterbrook Lane, stressing just how life-and-death our situation had become. This dolorous exhortation hit her crucifying canine between the eyes. As the agitated appeal drifted closer, Mum's face morphed into that of a helpless baby. Tranquillising teardrops welled up in her tormented fawn-eyes and with each liberating sob she loosened her pernicious pooch's leash. Trembling with trepidation, she succumbed to the butty of bliss.

Moved by her enraptured, haggard face, I recalled how we'd slathered our buttery croissants with confiture in her favoured Parisian café. Was this a glimpse of that self-confident feisty woman? Strawberry-smeared hugs and kisses ensued before she was stretchered into the ambulance by two gregarious paramedics. As we were blue-lighted away from Heartsease, I wondered whether her detestable dog really had been unleashed, or whether it would still be yapping at our heels?

Like all the King's horses and all the King's men, the junior doctor at Westbourne General casualty department couldn't reassemble Mum's fragile smashed soul. Expounding on hospital politics, he speedily stitched up Mum's battle scar without once mentioning her striking scrawniness. We were discharged post-haste with me in a piebald flap about Mum's delicate recovery.

However, my stout-hearted sliver had astounded me over the past week. Yes, there had been squabbles over spaghetti servings, jogging jiggery-pokery and milk-diluting manipulation; but my strong little shoot was beginning to sprout. With all the chatter and chuckles of long-separated companions, we contorted ourselves through a game of Twister, baked cheese scones together and planned a trip to the Courtauld Gallery for when Mum was blooming. There was even mention of the dreaded 'double d' words, prompting yet more soothing snivels and cherished memories of our mutual idol. It finally felt like she was biting the disgusting dog that bit her, even if it was hard to stomach.

Whilst I knew it wouldn't be a silver bullet, with luck the skylark necklace would be a moving memento for Mum. Perhaps she would feel more resilient knowing that a scintilla of Dad was there to escort her through life's assault course.

Stepping out under the summery seersucker sky, I craved another adventure within the green arabesque tapestry of the valley. After last week's death slide, I pined to be nestled in the sheltered bower of Dad's beautiful beech. Today I would luckily get my chance. Kate, an old friend from university, was coming to spend the day with Mum. Now in remission from her breast cancer, she was acutely sensitive to the roily rock-strewn road we'd been bludgeoned into trekking along over the past year.

There'd been some piebald pestering as I'd packed up my rucksack for the respite mission. Magpie mockery accompanied my packed lunch preparations. Would Mum touch the extra round of sandwiches I'd left in the fridge for her? And unearthing Dad's prized binoculars had been downright decadence in my magpie's stern Stygian eyes.

I found Mum under the silver birch, leafing through photo albums and nursing a peppermint tea.

'Oh, there you are! I wondered where you'd got to. Gorgeous day, isn't it?' I nattered inoffensively, keen to avoid a farewell fracas.

'Hi, love. Not a cloud in the sky, it's lovely. I fancied a trip down memory lane. Don't you look young in this one here!' Mum reminisced, stroking longingly a beaming snap of us all at Banthorpe Cove.

'So do you!' I enthused, admiring Mum's healthy bikini-clad body. With her auburn hair swept up in a messy chignon and her tanned peachy skin, she'd been effortlessly attractive.

'Those were the best kind of days. Do you remember burying Dad in the sand, or the games of frisbee, or our rockpooling expeditions?' Mum gushed, twinkling at the fond halcyon recollections. 'And boy, those blackcurrant-ripple ice creams were good! It was a nightmare trying to prise you away from the waves, you so loved your bodyboarding!'

'When we got back to the car covered in sand and with the ozone in our nostrils, we knew we'd had fun!' I babbled, picturing us contentedly weary from a full day at the beach. 'I could have spent all day in the water, riding the surf with Dad.'

'It seems like only yesterday. Oh, to be back there having fun together!' Mum yearned wistfully, bitter tears of remembrance pricking her eyelids.

'Maybe we could book a little Devon pilgrimage for half-term?' I suggested, eager to retain the optimistic atmosphere. 'October would be quieter and cheaper.'

'It wouldn't be the same, though,' whimpered a downhearted Mum, fiddling with her blouse buttons as a distraction from her distressing thoughts.

'But we can create new memories, Mum,' I proposed reassuringly, huddling up beside her and caressing her angular shoulders. Sanguine or not, I had to pretend to be for Mum's sake.

'Look what I've discovered,' I added tantalisingly, fishing out the claret leather box from my trouser pocket and handing it to Mum.

'A parting gift for you,' I uttered expectantly, watching her face light up at the loyal lucky charm.

Fondling the shimmering skylark, she let her grief bubble over.

I viewed these uncharacteristic eruptions of emotion as progress. Tougher than I'd cared to realise, she'd weathered the storm of last week and was now starting to warble, even if she was yet to spread her wings. Clasped around her décolletage like

Grandpa's lifeline pendant, I hoped she'd be equipped to soar through life's alarm calls.

'I'll always associate skylarks with Dad,' she blubbed, twiddling with the silvery chain. 'Their songs uplift me just like he did.'

Itching to tell me the whole cathartic story, she continued with tears cascading down her prominent cheekbones: 'It was in the Cotswolds that I first heard them. When we were courting, Dad whisked me away for a romantic break. Typical Dad, though, we'd gone off the beaten track on an adventure. Hand in hand in the middle of a squelchy cornfield we heard their bright tune. I'd never listened to anything more beautiful.'

I embraced her protectively, longing that she could share in my adventure and allow the whispers of the Washwell to reawaken her. But her canine oppressor wouldn't yet authorise such frivolous loss of control. She'd brought her hectoring hound to heel, but it still wasn't Crufts' agility champion.

'Are you sure you don't want me to stay?' I queried, pied prickles of penitence prodding at my own eyes.

'No, no, you go and have some fun. It'll do you good. Anyway, Kate will be here soon,' she insisted, as if sentenced to a lifetime of amusement abstinence.

'Alright then, as long as you're sure. Hope you have a good chinwag with Kate. I've left some sandwiches in the fridge, and I'm very happy to make dinner when I get back,' I prattled, anxious to avoid a rebellion-inducing 'take care of yourself' lecture.

'Bye, sweetie,' she enthused, struggling to flex her gangly limbs enough to embrace me. 'I'll look forward to hearing all about your exciting escapades later!'

I held her close and hoped I wasn't being honeyfuggled. Too many times her guileful greyhound had got the better of her. Would she be brave enough to bark back at it?

'Love you, Mum!' I chirruped, setting off apprehensively down the driveway.

I latched the gate and waved animatedly back at my silver-tongued scrap, my piebald menace persistently pleading me to stay. But I set off down the lane, intent on answering back to my avian intimidator. It had been a full-on week and I needed breathing space.

I attempted to admire the amber clusters of smiling silverweed. I endeavoured to listen to the cheerful chitters of a welcoming woodlark. But what if Kate was hoodwinked by Mum's cunning canine? And would there be some get-out clause for lunch? Imagine if Kate left early, giving Mum the opportunity to sneak in a gruelling run? With multiple magpie misgivings thrashing around in my head, the comforting contours of the countryside cuddled me closer.

I didn't anticipate a delirious déjà vu given the events of the past week. But back in the sylvan arms of my boosting beech, I felt secure. I nuzzled in to its moss-moled skin and drank in its invigorating petrichor scent. Shafts of warming sunlight filtered through its lime locks and brightened my broken body.

All of a sudden Rice Krispie crackles bounced off my enlivened eardrums. Sputters of sensation fizzed in my excited ear canals. Goosebumps of gratification made my sweating skin shiver. Could lightning really strike my lugholes twice? Perhaps last week's cunicular capers weren't just a fanciful fantasy? Impatient to find out, I scampered off ebulliently along the root-plaited pathway, just like my lively leporine playmates.

Unloading my black-and-white burden with each serene skip, I craved another rapturous rabbit rendezvous. Or would my astonishing ability extend to other articulate animals that I happened upon? Twinkles of warmth waltzed around the brindled bridleway ballroom. Puffball marshmallows spectated from the fern-fringed sidelines. A robin hidden in its oak minstrel's gallery twittered its 'Blue Danube' ditty.

The persistent purring now pulsed through my entire body. But it had been a pretty fraught week and maybe I needed to loosen up to hear the lilting lullabies of the valley. Reaching a junction, I plumped upon the left-hand fork which appeared to wind deeper into the pea-green paisley jungle.

My ears brimmed with blaring buzzing as I meandered along the spangle-speckled footpath searching for chattering creatures. Around each bend I despairingly scoured the reticulated ravel of green for signs of prospective pals. Despite this woodland sanctuary swarming with life, traces of blathering beasts eluded me. Interrupting a clouded magpie moth resting on a branch of blackthorn, I fruitlessly followed its piebald flutters. My own magpie nemesis was clearly interference to the wavelength of the Washwell. I would heed Dad's tried and trusted adage and let coy nature come to me.

Presently I lighted upon a crane's bill-carpeted clearing in the bushy beech bulwark. Ahead, the sloping field opened out like a herringbone handkerchief. The matted mound was woven with a chevron stitch of pens, chicken-wire runs and feeders, and was bobbled with reams of cavorting pheasants. As I ventured out from my forest haven, my still-thrumming ears braced themselves for a rowdy gallinacean rave.

Advancing down the narrow hawthorn-hemmed field path, I grasped just how substantial a set-up this was. Up ahead, masses of spluttering pheasants swarmed hither and thither between line after line of wire-mesh cages. Was this another Hugo head-trip? A self-gratification scheme to woo his most lucrative clients as they spent an afternoon obliterating the local game bird population? Yes, these discombobulated zig-zagging lambs to the slaughter were unknowingly being fattened for Hugo's ego-fest.

I hungered for my auditory super ability to kick in. What were these flummoxed fowls squawking as they swerved aimlessly to and fro? And what was that beastly brouhaha as they performed their befuddled Lindy hop?

I struggled to keep up with their Screwball Scramble-swerves and startled leprechaun kicks. But approaching a gap in the hedgerow-rickrack, my whirring ears suddenly woke up with a jarring jolt.

'Hurry up, this way, please!' yawped a bossy-sounding hazel-freckled hen, marshalling her dull-witted troops through the aperture.

It was like watching throngs of Christmas shoppers jostling down the stairs of Oxford Street tube station, only with added gawkiness. Distinct voices were impossible to decipher within the deafening din. I opted to watch from afar, uncertain as to whether I wanted to hang around with these baffling birds. Hundreds of conceited cocks, humble hens and perplexed poults careened towards the chink with a clumsy kerfuffle. This was another level of hoggish Hugo excess. After lengthy mystified shepherding, I was keen to discover what all the fuss and feathers was about. Peeking through the opening with my trusty binoculars, I spied agape on the clamorous convention.

Addressing her bevy of buffoons from a moss-marbled stump, the officious sergeant major bellowed across the adjacent field:

'OK, Fasane, *hört mal zu!*'

Did a feeble-minded pheasant really possess the intellect to master German? Maybe I wouldn't stay if I needed a dictionary to decode this hurly-burly.

'Friends, Washwellites, countrybirds, lend me your ear tufts,' prattled the garrulous governor to her stirred, screeching swarm.

'Flap for the stars, comrades! Our day of glory is almost upon us. You too have the chance to shine in our epic krabfoodling extravaganza! But the early pheasant grabs the grain and today we'll be holding our first set of auditions. Have you got the Zwerp Factor?'

Clueless chants of 'Frau Strumpwaffle, Frau Strumpwaffle!' resounded across the valley.

'This is your big moment to strut your squawky stuff in front of our esteemed judging panel. Champion krabfoodlers will ultimately perform in our phenomenal pheasant pageant. And how about the opportunity to parade in front of our philanthropic providers, their explosive praise echoing around the valley? The krabfoodling knapweed crown is yours for the taking!' rhapsodised the fanatical, gesticulating chairpheasant Strumpwaffle, blissfully ignorant of game-shooting etiquette.

This certainly made the feathers fly. Feverish pheasants veered aimlessly around the mobbed meadow, their crazed clucks thronging the animated air. Like a symposium of frisky five year-olds, they pranced hither and thither, erupting at whim into shrieks of delirium. Dust-bathing and wing-waggling to flaunt their elation, my ears hurt at this hysterical hullabaloo. What the dickens was krabfoodling? And what's zwerping when it's at home? Would I learn anything constructive from spending time with these birdbrains? In any case, I was fast finding out that whilst speech is silver, sometimes silence is golden.

CHAPTER 6

# SIX FOR GOLD

'First to hit the zwerping piste is "in it to win it" Justin dancing his splutterfug shake,' trumpeted a zealous Frau Strumpwaffle to her rumbustious audience. 'Go for gold, J-bird!'

Cringing open-mouthed at this noisy nye of nitwits, I decided to watch their bizarre buffoonery from afar. From their mallow-fringed molehill rostrum, three po-faced pheasant adjudicators were poised to scrutinise the squawking contestants. A cacophonous gallinacean gaggle flocked chaotically around them. Frau Strumpwaffle was the excitable, ear-splitting compere. Caterpillar cornets and gummy grasshoppers were circulated by a befuddled usher to screeches of delight. A band of blockheads were tuning up for the surreal spectacle on their goat's-beard guitars and soapwort saxophones. But I'd never be able to make head nor tail of the absurd action with this interminable brassy bangarang.

'Button your beaks!' bawled a ruffled Frau Strumpwaffle, whirring her wings as an ineffective referee whistle.

From the sow thistle-swathed sidelines swaggered a supercilious cock to a spate of raucous jeering. Parading along the zwerping piste like a pompous peacock, Justin was evidently basking in his moment of glory. He flounced haughtily around, preening his sequined chestnut plumage and joggling his bronze-tinselled tail. Swanking about to ramp up the suspense, he jiggled his bottle-green top hat and waggled his permatan wattles. Infatuated hens squealed dotingly and pelted the prancing popinjay with moulted plumes. With his bumptious beak in the air, Justin thought the sun shined out of his resplendent tail feathers. For the sake of the other competitors, I very much hoped that this would be a case of all that glittered not being gold.

After all that ridiculous razzmatazz and much exasperated heckling for him to stop poncing around and get a zwerp on, Justin launched himself into the limelight with a strident splutter. He sashayed gracelessly hither and thither accompanied by dissonant dance ditties and the boisterous boos and hisses of the unimpressed horde. Alas, it appeared that this pretentious pinhead had been blessed with two left claws. I had to stifle my sniggers as he hurled himself to and fro with a salvo of clamorous jabbers. His priceless pièce de résistance was a cloddish catapult skyward, legs akimbo, to clattering chants of 'Krab-a-foodle-doo!' Still revelling in his macho megastardom and blind to his bungling, he flaunted and flailed his garish plumage as a self-enforced encore.

'Well, thank you, Justin, for that thoroughly, errr, diverting display!' yabbered Frau Strumpwaffle, feigning admiration for the clumsy, condescending cock. 'Prized pundits, what are the scores on the claws?'

An equally poncey poult strutted forward for his analysis: 'I'm afraid it's a measly three from me, Strumpy. Your zwerps need to be more controlled, Justin, and your krabfoodle lacked the pizzazz I'd expect for this level of competition. All in all, a bit of a cack-winged calamity if I'm honest!'

Steam was clearly coming out of Justin's emerald ear tufts, but he continued to rollick rowdily around like he ruled the roost.

The other highfalutin judges proceeded to tickpick his dire dance efforts. After his painful performance had been utterly ripped to shreds, Justin's final score was a paltry eight points. In spite of this, he flung himself into a dippy territorial display in an attempt to recover his pummelled pride.

'Next up is shrinking violet Suki dancing her cluckstep. Shake that tail feather, sister hen!' enthused Frau Strumpwaffle, doubtless keen to detract attention from the arrogant ass striding about in front of her.

Quaking behind a tussock of lilac-flecked toadflax was a timorous hen attempting to pluck up the courage to take centre stage. With her understated dun and buff plumage, gangly wrinkled legs and pale complexion, sheepish Suki was certainly no oil painting. Her tousled stubby tail was all tangled and her muted bill chattered with consternation in the weld-curtained wings. This chary humdrum hen was tearing her freckled feathers out as she scuttled frantically backwards and forwards, biding time. Pecking neurotically at some stray maize grains to steady her jittery nerves, she gingerly sidled onto the zwerping track with a flustered flap. I would silently egg on the underpheasant here; after all, she couldn't be as hopeless as risible exhibitionist Justin.

'Don't drag your claws! Get a wiggle on! Krabba-dabba-foodle!' taunted the tetchy, turbulent throng, further inhibiting self-conscious Suki.

With her heart in her beak, the bashful bird scurried frenziedly this way and that with a bewildered gibber. Was this skittish spontaneity or a higgledy-piggledy hash-up? The demented rabble certainly didn't know whether to laugh or cry and thus continued with their tumultuous twattle.

With all the finesse of a terpsichorean tortoise, Suki fumbled through her zig-zagging zwerps and floundered on her frightful fishtail turns. With heartless hectoring clanging in her hypersensitive ear tufts, she stumbled all a flutter into her catastrophic krabfoodle car crash. This was less pirouetting prima ballerina and more muddled morris dancer. Mortified at her maladroitness, she beetled off meekly into the rowdy rumpus looking somewhat down in the beak.

'Wow, Suki, you surpassed yourself with that, umm, most unusual and edifying execution of the cluckstep!' blabbered Frau Strumpwaffle, buttoning her bill on the tottering tragedy. 'Krabfoodle connoisseurs, how's that holly leaf leaderboard looking?'

An immaculately preened no-nonsense judge limbered up for her scathing audit of angst-ridden Suki's dance debacle. The ham-clawed hen cowered diffidently in the shaded meadow corner, steeling herself for the panning.

'Krabfoodle chaos! It's a four and no more for that zwerpshambles. Fine feathers make fine birds – frumpish dull plumage won't get you anywhere, my dear…'

I was thankfully rescued from this freakish pheasant farce by a battered jolting jeep stuttering down the field. Baffled bedlam ensued with a swarm of clamorous cretins skedaddling here, there and everywhere.

Strictly for the birds, krabfoodling had taught me nothing other than that laughter is often the best medicine in life. But the surreal zwerping spectacular had nonetheless confirmed that pheasants were the avian world's daftest most deafening members.

Staggering out of the old banger was Hugo's hunched scapegoat whistling a carefree tune. Ensconced within the lulling landscape, my fellow Atlas seemed thrilled to have escaped his roguish tormentor. But as he hobbled wearily towards me, it became apparent that this downtrodden doormat had been ground down by Hugo's brutish bullying.

The trampled skivvy doddered along the field edge scanning the pens, every now and again clutching his back and wincing in pain. I presumed this lurching lackey was Hugo's gamekeeper as I watched him diligently inspecting feeder levels and hirpling in and out of a dilapidated lean-to for additional supplies. As he shuffled along the row of cages nearest to me, I took in his sapped, weather-beaten face. This was Mr. Bellington-Fraser's predictable goldbricking – wowing his valued clientele with a shoot masterminded single-handedly by this hapless sitting target. Trundling torturously in my direction, I reached out to the tyrannised stooge with a convivial smile.

'Fine morning for a pootle, missy,' nattered the genial gamekeeper, doffing his corduroy flat cap.

'It's beautiful, isn't it?' I replied, eager to show this dedicated dogsbody that somebody cared.

'Mungo Dunthorpe's me name. Pleased to meet you, lass,' he chattered courteously, proffering a grubby wizened hand.

'And you. I'm Ella,' I said, affably shaking his outstretched earth-caked hand. 'We've just moved in to a little bungalow on the other side of the valley. It's great for exploring around here!'

'Welcome to the Washwell! Most scrumptious part of the world, if you ask me. Daresay you've had a gander at Socknersh Manor on your mosey? Well, Mr. Bellington-Fraser's the new squire and I'm his estate manager. Always running round like a headless hen, that's me!

'Doing a spot of twitching, are you, Miss?' he asked, motioning to Dad's treasured binoculars which were hung around my neck.

'Yes, I'm a bit of a nature nut. I always feel a million times better when I'm outside. The wildlife's astounding around here!' I raved, unable to convey just how out-of-this-world nature had become for me. I'd just witnessed a whacky gallinacean talent contest, for goodness' sake! My jingling ears were still recovering from the perplexing pandemonium.

Winking and grinning and with a twinkle in his kindly crow's-footed eyes, he whispered:

'If you're a birder, lassie, then there's a falcon nesting in the field o'er yonder. Made its home in the old folly. Bootiful creature!

Not so good for me pheasants, mind you – partial to a few eggs or even poults, you see. But I won't tell Mr. B-F if you won't, eh?'

Before I'd had a chance to process what he'd divulged, he babbled on: 'Still, better than them darn maggoty pies. Always trying to snaffle eggs, pesky rotters! Varmints, that's what they is! Well, I'd best be off – no rest for the wicked and all that. Otherwise Mr. B-F'll have me guts for garters! I'll be seeing yer round, no doubt.'

'Bye! Lovely to have met you!' I called, watching him limp awkwardly down the field for his next chore.

I found it somewhat ironic that this exploited altruist had the initials 'MD'. Whilst Hugo liked to think of himself as the heroic top dog, this sedulous salt of the earth was actually the managing director of the Bellington-Fraser operation. I wondered if, just like Dad, myrmidon Mungo was the victim of his own dedication. In any case, I felt a strange affinity for this magpie-loathing avuncular countryman and hoped that we would cross paths again.

Snapping, crackling and popping furiously, my expectant ears were searching for the next wild adventure. Would I catch a glimpse of the magnificent falcon that Mungo had mentioned? Might it even be a peregrine? If it found its voice, what would it say to me? And what would a falcon's foibles and fancies be?

With this exciting prospect in my bustling brain, I set forth back up the field with a spring in my step. Zippily zig-zagging along the rutted footpath, I tittered imagining the next pheasant failure spluttering onto the zwerp floor. Nestled in the hawthorn purfle, a party of pearly ox-eye daisies smiled back at me. A guffawing green woodpecker had evidently observed the hilarious havoc too. But whilst it had undoubtedly been entertaining escapism, I wasn't sure my ears could endure another gallinacean rendezvous any time soon.

Back amongst the crimson crane's bill carpet, I was glad to be cosseted by my beech blanket once more. Spotting a conveniently located timber stack trestle table, I perched on a stump seat and pulled out my packed lunch. As I tucked in to my squished rounds of cheese and pickle, I hoped that Mum's hadn't been craftily flushed down the toilet. With luck, the morning had been more about chummy chinwag and our specially baked cherry cake than her conniving canine.

Gradually, I made out the discordant drift of tuneless caterwauling heading towards me. This mockery of a melody was suddenly interrupted by an approaching conversation.

'Well, we won't reserve your place in the Brock and Roll Hall of Fame just yet then, love!' joshed an affectionate female voice, chuckling gently.

'My ears are all a jangle thanks to your tone-deafness, Hil!' she continued playfully, now seemingly about to cross my path.

'Sorry, Colly! You know I love a bit of the White Stripes. I just couldn't help myself! Or maybe you'd prefer my rendition of "Going Underground"?' a male companion tenderly teased.

Squinting in the sunlight-streaked clearing, I finally clapped my incredulous eyes on the nearing natterers. Sauntering chirpily towards me in their Breton-striped berets were a pair of silvery badgers. But surely they were nocturnal? I remembered how Dad had set up an infrared camera in Nana and Grandpa's garden to observe them. We'd chortled at their gleeful fruit-gobbling antics and even seen their pawprints in the sandpit come dawn! Still, anything seemed plausible given the last fortnight's boisterous bunnies and foolish pheasants.

'What's that up ahead, dearest? It's all gone a bit blurry again!' fretted the apprehensive hoary sow, clutching hold of her male companion for reassurance. 'Please don't say they've got a whumpstick! I'll be all of a doodah if there's another horrid bang! And my knees just won't tolerate another crazy chase. I'm not a young whippersnapper anymore, you know!'

Pausing to give his female friend a supportive nuzzle, the smoky big-hearted boar warily eyed me up. To avoid a meline meltdown, perhaps it would help to introduce myself to this doting duo?

'My name's Ella. Pleased to meet you both. What a lovely day it is!' I ventured, keen to soothe these endearing soulmates.

Their discombobulated expressions reflected my own feelings on this bizarre situation, but they heaved sighs of relief that I wasn't a foe.

'It's alright my lovely, she's a honeycub. Nothing to fear here, and no whumpsticks to boot!' exclaimed the benevolent boar, planting a loving kiss on the pawwringer's furry cheek.

'It's a pleasure to meet you, my dear! I'm Hilaire and this is my wonderful wife Colette. Twelve years she's put up with me and my DIY disasters, you know! The happiest of my life, mind you. Cracking mum to our four cubs as well. Don't know what I'd do without her!' he effused, placing a protective paw around his worrying wife's shoulder.

'Hello there, lovey. He's a big softie, really, even if he did almost saw off his paw bodging together our brackenbramble settee!' Colette recalled, smirking and burying her face in her paws in mock despair.

'We were just off for a spot of joydling if you fancied tagging along?' invited an enthusiastic Hilaire, rubbing his itchy paws along the log pile. 'Always cheers us up if we're feeling a bit long-faced!'

'Sounds good to me!' I effervesced, uncertain what I was letting myself in for. But the day was still young and this devoted double act reminded me uncannily of my precious parents. Besides, joydling sounded like it could only be a beneficial way to spend an afternoon.

We began ambling along the bracken-bordered footpath, the badgers occasionally resting to scratch their claws and rub their ivory underbellies on dappled beech backscratchers. Watching them guzzle on succulent snowberries for sustenance, there was definitely still vim in these hale and hearty treasures.

'Colette's a bit of a creative whizz in the joydle, although she's too modest to admit it!' extolled Hilaire, rolling around the rutted track in excitement. 'We're almost there now – prepare to be flabbergasted, ma chérie!'

'Excuse my husband, he's like a cub in a honey hive!' tutted a blushing Colette, palling up with me for a girly natter. 'I do apologise for my hysterical hissy fit earlier, by the way. We've had a couple of terrifying incidents recently, you see. One time we'd popped down to Badgens for some eggs to go with our earthworm sausages. Hilaire loves a good fry-up! It was jam-packed with those rowdy birds swerving in and out of the aisles, almost knocked us off our paws, the rascals!

'All of a sudden there was a blasting boom and a man with a whumpstick and a vile skinny dog pursued us up the trolley ramp. My eyes have never been that good, but this roaring dark stranger stank something rotten! Muttering on about his cows and his prized birds as Hilaire snarled at him he was, the nasty bit of work! I've been petrified ever since!' she rattled, shuddering at the harrowing memory and snuggling in to Hilaire's grey-haired chest.

'There, there, darling. It made my fur creep too. But the final unbearable straw was seeing our dear daughter Geneviève imprisoned in the supermarket snare. Luckily she managed to break free within the day, but it was torture watching her trapped and wasting away like that,' Hilaire sobbed, drawing his trembling wife closer for succour.

Hugo's relentless reign of terror seemingly dragged on. Their ordeal only added fuel to my Bellington-Fraser-hating fire. After all, I knew too well the traumatic trials and tribulations of suffering a loved one disappear before your very eyes. In silent contemplation, they quickened their plodding pace around the next bindweed-braided bend, eager to show me their pride and joy.

Presently we reached a glistening gilded glade within the mottled beech mélange. This delightful dazzling dell was dusted with drifts of golden blooms. My ecstatic eyes were spellbound by garlands of gleaming goldenrod, tuffets of flaxen mignonette and bright bouquets of aureate tansy. A glittering sprinkle of resplendent ragwort had been added for good measure.

I was given an exuberant tour of the burgeoning vegetable patch crammed full with sparkling swathes of lemony wild parsnip, twinkling tussocks of wintercress and blonde clusters of shimmering wood sage. What a joyous sight to behold! Who knew that instead of resting, badgers gardened during the day?

'It's heavenly! You've created something very special here,' I wholeheartedly exclaimed, pausing to appreciate a glistering posy of amber agrimony.

'Oh, it's nothing, really. Our haven does bring us a great deal of happiness, though. Sorry it's a bit, errr, yellow. You see, with our poor eyesight we need a vivid colour scheme,' explained a self-effacing rosy-cheeked Colette.

'Yellow's a rather hopeful colour, I find,' added a ruminative, optimistic Hilaire. 'The hue of a warm summer's day and hardy springtide primroses.'

Perched on a fallen moss-marbled tree, I avidly contemplated them tending their labour of love. With their snouts to the grindstone, they were a template of conscientious teamwork. A spirited Hilaire was on digging duties, whilst a now-calm Colette was chief prettifier.

Grateful tears trickled down my glowing cheeks as I glimpsed them meticulously grooming each other with adoring looks in their effulgent eyes. Snuggling up together on a beaming bed of wild pansies, these golden-hearted gems settled down for a well-earned snooze. They'd helpfully shown me that if you looked hard enough, glimmers of gold could shine through the black-and-white patches of life.

CHAPTER 7

# SEVEN FOR A SECRET YET TO BE TOLD

Enthroned triumphantly atop Hugo's vile victory arch perched a noble, ermine-robed peregrine. Surveying the wooded whale-backed Washwell with its scintillating obsidian eyes, its opalescent Prussian blue plumage glistened in the serene afternoon sunlight. With one of its golden talons drawn up to its coppery velvet cape, this majestic, moustachioed specimen was indulging in a spot of regal relaxation. Alas, the fine shimmer-freckled falcon was steadfastly holding its peace.

Like a soggy cereal grain, perhaps my auditory superpower was fizzling out? Mind you, I'd certainly had my fair share of aural adventures today. Exhausted from their unorthodox work-out, my ears were nonetheless still softly sputtering. But the breathtaking bird could only muster its customary 'kak-kak' call. Swallowing my disappointment, I watched awestruck as it swiftly glided off into the sparkling viridine valley. As I marvelled at its sleek slate-blue body deftly stooping on an unsuspecting snack, I hoped that next time it might find its voice.

Plotting out the homeward journey on my rain-wrinkled OS map, I opted for a meandering route which would pass the charmingly titled Glydwish Farm. My unmanacled mind brimmed with radiant recollections as I sallied ebulliently forth into the susurrating sage sward.

The field was fringed with a gilded garnish of jaunty buttercups, merrily evoking both jovial, joggletailing frolics and today's golden horticultural haven. A distant pheasant's clamorous krabfoodle-splurt made me cackle like a kookaburra at the thought of poseur Justin being catapulted cacophonously heavenward. With luck, these extraordinary animal encounters would be the first of many intrepid explorations of this wondrous wilderness.

'Capital afternoon, eh, what?' remarked a posh, assertive voice behind me.

Spinning round to determine my pursuer, I was greeted with the glinting amber eyes of a scurrying rufous fox. So my ears were still in the offbeat groove after all!

'Must dash, young miss! Lady wife's cooking Sunday roast for the family. Sorted the chicken this morning, now on a wild goose chase for the spuds. Got to love a roast potato dripping in duck fat, eh! Don't want to disappoint my dear vixen. Toodle-pip, fine filly!' gabbled the nimble tod, hightailing it down the meadow before I'd had a chance to reply.

Another auditory anticlimax left me feeling rather crestfallen. Perhaps my still-thrumming ears were understandably exhausted from their eccentricity overload?

Oh, how I wished that roast potatoes weren't Mum's fear food! A roast dinner would be my desert island meal and I'd missed Dad's divine crispy King Edwards each Sunday. Until Mum could be more carb-courageous, tonight I'd have to rustle up something which didn't send her, or me, into a piebald potato panic.

But my attention was now diverted to the approaching higgledy-piggledy farmstead. The footpath snaked between the motley mishmash of dilapidated outbuildings. Wrestling with a rickety iron gate hung haphazardly from its rusty hinges, I took in every decrepit detail of this sad shambles. A flaky pebbledash cottage was the crumbling tumbledown centrepiece, although a blushing pink rose was rambling vigorously around the scuffed front door.

Dodging the tatty jumble of clapped-out farm machinery strewn pell-mell over the raggedy farmyard, I pondered whether exploitation was at play once more. The maroon 'BF' emblazoned on each ramshackle gate stressed that this was unquestionably Bellington-Fraser property. I pitied the unfortunate tenant lumbered with this topsy-turvy tangle and squeezed dry by our heartless whip-cracker extraordinaire. Threading my way around the final battle-scarred barn, I longed to get back to my uplifting utopia.

The restorative breeze soothed my seething flushed skin as I headed for the nettle-trimmed kissing-gate in the field's sylvan seam. Having exited the stallionback and now protected under the green argyle arbour of a sinuous sunken track, my ears immediately stopped buzzing.

A yawning blonde evening primrose hinted that Mum's dinner was looming – I'd hopefully be back for more natural nourishment tomorrow. Winding down the gnarly fleabane-fringed track, I relished the sublime cool calmness. Mottles of twilight filtered through the greenwood gossamer and illuminated the cerise straggles of ragged robin which lined my root-plaited path. The fruity fragrance of heady honeysuckle filled the mellifluously murmuring air.

Descending further into this delightful sanctuary, I noticed a lofty male figure sauntering towards me. Too dignified and too rangy for Hugo, I took in this salmon-shirted stranger. His leaden-footed strides and pensive expression suggested something was preying on his mind. The least I could do was to pass the time of day with him.

'Lovely evening for a stroll!' I chattered amiably, keen to perk up this brooding giant.

'Mmm,' mumbled the tanned ruminator, his thoughts clearly elsewhere.

'Are you alright?' I chanced, empathising with the melancholy muser.

'Oh, hullo there. I do apologise, million miles away today. Touch of bad news, you see. Still, stiff upper lip and all that! Roly St. Clare,' he prattled, extending a bronzed tremulous hand. 'Farm up at Glydwish. You probably rambled through earlier. Jolly pleased to meet you.'

'Hi, I'm Ella. We've just moved to the area. It must be wonderful farming this stunning landscape!' I enthused, eager to foster a cheery atmosphere.

At this, his turquoise blood-shot eyes became downcast once more.

'Couple of years ago now we came to Glydwish. It was *my* hare-brained scheme to live the good life. Brassed off with the humdrum of city stockbroking, you see. Wife loved the Washwell. Spiffing at the start, even if it was bloody hard graft!

'All gone a bit to pot now, mind you, what with the measly milk price and the rent and the endless extortionate repairs. And now the new landlord has his sights on a beastly mega-dairy for our beloved Friesians! Jolly galling, if truth be told!' he offloaded, wringing his hands all the while. 'Still, mustn't wang on, sups is calling!'

'Sorry it's all a bit tough at the moment,' I commiserated, unsure how to react to this endearing, jabbering bundle of nerves.

'Anyhow, need to check on my dear Harriet. She's with calf, you see. Not coping well with this heat, mind you, what with her varicose veins and all that. And there's still the wheat to harvest before sundown too. Must scoot! Pip pip!' he babbled, scrambling speedily off into the burbling hazy evening.

'Bye! Nice to have met you!' I called, observing his twitchy lank frame darting through the dusk-dappled kissing gate.

This added yet another spark to my Bellington-Fraser bushfire. Incandescent with fury, I stormed down the remainder of the serpentine pathway, a ground-elder icing sugar dusted liberally over the moss-matted banks. The harsh, guttural trill of an insistent starling echoed the wrathful mutters of my mind. A pungent stubbly straggle of black horehound marked the end of the jade-thatched footpath.

Face to frightful face with the brash eyesore of Socknersh, I hankered after revenge for Dad and for all the allies I'd had the pleasure of meeting. Thankful to emerge into the calming calamine crepuscule, I began my homeward trek.

I was greeted with a smouldering saffron sunset as my weary feet trudged up our driveway. Clandestine canine capers hopefully hadn't scuppered Kate's visit and Mum would be in high spirits. Part of me was desperate to divulge my astonishing animal adventures to her, but for the moment I would keep schtum. Breathing in my final fortifying lungfuls of ambrosial agrarian air, I anticipated what exciting escapades tomorrow would bring.

Nestled in Dad's teal velvet beanbag, I found Mum painting her toenails in her floral pyjamas. With a couple of chocolate digestives and a glass of milk beside her, she looked more chilled out than she had done for a long while. And when was the last time she'd taken this much pride in her appearance? It was all looking rather promising. Perhaps the silver skylark *had* been the miraculous motivation she'd needed?

'Hi, love, how's you? Can't wait to hear all about your intrepid exploring!' she gushed, screwing the bottle of scarlet nail polish shut and beaming up at me.

'Hey, Mum. I'm totally bushed, but it was a wonderful day, thanks. How about you, did you have a good catch-up with Kate?' I enquired, hoping there hadn't been any hellhound hassles.

'It was fab, thank you. Just what I needed. I won't bore you with the details, though, I'm sure you've got loads of exciting stories to tell me,' she uttered, rolling the shimmering skylark between her thumb and forefinger. Why did her pestilent pooch always insist on any perceived pleasure being played down? Her day mattered just as much as mine.

Hungrily hurrying to the newly christened biscuit barrel, I helped myself to a handful of melty moreishness and flopped on the gratifyingly comfortable sofa beside Mum. I regaled her with thrilling tales of my rural rendezvous, obviously omitting the implausible auditory accompaniments. Bravely, and dare I say it contentedly, devouring her biscuits and milk, she listened attentively as I recounted stories of farcical pheasants, bewitching badgers and the phenomenal falcon climax.

But Mum clearly wasn't in a loquacious mood. She seemed upbeat enough; perhaps she was just drained from her day. Or maybe she was peckish; after all, we still had a great many hound-shaped hurdles to leap over. All the same, a few months ago I would have done anything to get back even a smidgen of the happier, hardier fighter that was now blossoming before me.

Aside from a custard contretemps, dinner had passed without undue canine kerfuffle. We'd chattered through the washing up and unwound with a hilarious episode of *Gogglebox* and Mum thrashing me at Scrabble. Her brain had most certainly not shrunk, even if her body had!

Drowsy from my diverse day, but for once not dog-tired, I retired to my room overflowing with optimism. Switching on my lotus flower lamp, I noticed a WhatsApp notification on my phone. It was from a concerned Kate. Propelled into a petrified piebald flap, my disillusioned eyes hastily scanned her considerate message:

*Hope you're well, Ella? Just checking your mum's recovered from her migraine – I know how crippling they can be. Let her know that I'm thinking of her. I'd love to see you both (and your dreamy new house!) as soon as possible. Take care, Kate xxxxxx*

So Mum's guileful greyhound *had* got the better of her after all! Should I confront her about this canine chicanery? Or was it better to let sleeping dogs lie? I'd make a decision in the cold, with luck corvid-free, light of day. My now-beat head sank back onto my squishy pillow, following the lead of my heavy heart.

*

The tenebrous tranquillity of entrancing Trolliloes was the perfect foil to the previous evening's disenchanting exposé. A succouring squeeze of Dad's beauteous beech had sent my ears into a tumultuous tintinnabulating full peal. Yearning for another glorious glimpse of the regal hematite tercel, I bounded briskly towards the rust-riddled kissing gate leading out to the folly field.

The unfortunate triumph of experience over hope had given way to allowing Mum a second chance. She had, after all, been making significant progress and maybe yesterday she'd needed the opportunity to catch up with her fragile soul. So I'd left her at her full organisational best, arranging scarves in her new wardrobe and crooning to Dad's Motown albums. She'd even had an extra slice of toast at breakfast and suggested she'd concoct a surprise dessert for dinner. A fluttering carousel of holly blue butterflies and the gold-dusted gorse bush embellishing the geriatric gate were imploring me to hold out hope.

Perched on a pretentious pillar of the neoclassical carbuncle, I excitedly anticipated the opulent, obsidian-eyed falcon. Cacophonous clanging still reverberated around my expectant ear canals as I delighted in the iridescent peridot patchwork of the Washwell.

The forceful flapping of wings followed by a controlled landing abruptly distracted me from the glimmering gallimaufry. Craning upwards to reveal my avian visitor, I was slightly miffed at the discovery of a brindled buzzard resting upon an ornate swan's neck pediment. I delved into my rucksack for my binoculars to have a closer inspection. Hunched on his grandiose watchtower, his gimlet umber eyes digested each minute detail of the pastoral parchment unfurled before him. With his muted mousy plumage and ivory chest insignia, he was the less impressive sombre cousin of my peregrine paragon.

His loftier stature seemed to be accompanied with an equally inflated opinion of self. Punctiliously preening his fawn feathers, this bumptious-looking bird arrogantly assumed that *he* ruled the rather flashy roost.

We were presently joined by a larger caramel-coloured female companion who settled atop an elaborate Corinthian column. She shuffled her razor-sharp xanthic talons along the poncey perch whilst vainly ruffling her pale barred plumes.

'A paradigm of the pastoral panegyric, don't you think, Demi?' mooted the meditative male, looking rather smug at his use of alliteration.

'Yes, the valley personally summoned up stanzas of Dylan Thomas's "Fern Hill",' propounded the highbrow hazel hen, as if to upstage her erudite rival.

'And such effective use of arboreal anadiplosis between fields!' eulogised the educated egotist, strutting along a sinuous marble scroll.

'Well, for me it was all about the oak tree epizeuxis and the clever hedgerow chiasmus!' raved the camel-coloured contemplator, going into raptures over something or other.

'In summary, a veristic bucolic aubade to the Washwell!' gloated the irritating clever Dick, swooping down to the grass for some earthworm brain fuel, closely followed by his fellow avian academic.

The buteonine brainboxes proceeded to swank around whilst extolling the virtues of Christopher Marlowe's 'The Passionate Shepherd to His Love', quite blind to the presence of a lesser mortal. Peacocking around like they were appearing on a special

Mensa-edition of *Mastermind*, I sniggered trying to make heads or tails of the high-flown intellectual waffle.

Mere muggle that I was, I eventually managed to decipher that they'd been wheeling above the landscape and 'reading' it like a poem. They were now intent on boastfully dissecting it to the nth degree in order to substantiate their brilliance. Maybe an incessant droning was more melodious than being subjected to this scholarly gobbledygook?

'Good day, young lady!' exclaimed the bookish brunette male, finally acknowledging my existence. Before I'd been granted the opportunity to reply, he ploughed on, clearly savouring the sound of his own vainglorious voice: 'Piedmont Buteo at your service. And this is my esteemed consort and colleague, Demelza. We've just been revelling in a touch of wheeding. Marvellous pursuit! Just as a matter of interest, what would your view of the Corneillesque château caesura be?'

All this brainy balderdash had brought me out in a cold sweat. It felt like I was out of my depth in an abstruse English literature exam. Struggling to even grasp the taxing *University Challenge*-style question, I plumped for the more customary salutation amongst the humble hoi-polloi: 'Hello there! My name's Ella. Pleased to meet you both.'

'Good morning, Miss. Fine day for an in-depth analysis! Such apposite use of ash tree anaphora within this variquoise vale, don't you find?' goaded the donnish goldstockinged Demelza, impatient to wheedle some astute witticism from me.

All hawk eyes were on me. Immobilised in my apparent ignorance, I ached to outsmart them with a novel nugget of wisdom. Now whispering behind my back, I sensed that I'd been excluded from their esoteric elite. Did I actually give two hoots? Not really, but their cerebral chauvinism was rather churlish.

It was, however, giving me an insightful appreciation of how Mum might be feeling. As the misunderstood, malnourished misfit, she too was striving to get her voice heard whilst battling against her ostracising greyhound. How suffocating to feel as if you were always unjustly being judged by your cover! How disabling to always be competing with a controlling, supercilious voice!

Although it was tempting to leave these exasperating eggheads disappearing up their own tail feathers, I chose to stay as an exercise in empathy. Besides, their posey pomposity was cracking me up. In any case, I longed for the peerless peregrine to return and knock them off their fancy-pants perch.

CHAPTER 8

# EIGHT FOR A WISH

D esperate to dodge the barrage of fiendish bullets being fired in my direction, I decided to give them a dose of their own distasteful medicine. After all, I might as well try and glean something useful from these learned loudbeaks. Clambering up a craggy Dartmoor tor, I remembered how Dad and I had witnessed a buzzard being harassed by a meddlesome magpie. Perhaps this cultivated couple could divulge some valuable tips for thwarting my piebald pest.

'How do you stop a magpie mobbing your mind?' I enquired, yearning for a cerebral ceasefire.

'What the devil is a magpie?' asked a for-once-flummoxed Piedmont, fluttering frustratedly back up to his pontifical perch to restore his supremacy.

I couldn't help feeling rather self-satisfied that I'd managed to outsmart these sententious swaggerers. Now that the boot was on the other claw, these wheeling dictionaries were evidently a bit browned off. Demelza pecked irately at the sun-baked earth and with his cere knocked out of joint, Piedmont haughtily ruffled his fuscous feathers.

I'd revel a moment in my smart-alec status: 'Oh, I do apologise! Let me describe one for you. They're a black-and-white bird in the corvid family. Scientific name is *Pica pica*. Incessantly chattering or contemptuously cackling at—'

'Ah, a pianet! Those pestiferous piebald pariahs! Always prating poppycock! And such dreadful philistines,' exclaimed Piedmont victoriously, clearly relieved to have recaptured the intellectual high ground. Even if it was my nefarious nemesis, I understood why a magpie might relish tormenting these stuck-up smarty pants.

'The last time we encountered those loathly boorish birds was above the frightful pheasant fleapit. That gauche gallinacean gaggle was staging an egregiously amateur performance of Rossini's *The Thieving Magpie*. A posse of pied preeners had gatecrashed the talon-curling fiasco. Shocked at the omnishambles, our revered compeer Valentino couldn't bite his beak any longer and took it upon himself to intervene,' gabbled a rattled Demelza, all a flutter about the indelible affair.

'Clamorous confusion ensued as the cretinous cast and their equally obtuse audience flailed hither and thither. The vexatious vermin then began their assault, besieging us three musketeers with all their black-and-white brutality. Of course, none of these brainless barbarians could rise to our dizzying heights. My advice to you, dear girl, is to always ensure you're soaring higher than your tormentor, then it will never be able to drag you down. Whatever you do, never deign to stoop to its lowly level!'

At this, Piedmont was uncharacteristically tight-beaked, hanging his mousy mortarboarded head in obvious distress.

Despite all the verbiage, the poignant punchline of the burbled yarn was a serendipitous godsend. A helpful reminder that if I wanted to fly, I had to cast aside *everything* that was weighing me down. My harassed mind now hatched from its imprisoning piebald shell, I'd possibly taken my first tentative flutters in the past few days. My overwhelming wish was that, in time, both Mum and I would be able to rise high into the emancipating cerulean skies, leaving our pitiless persecutors far below us.

'Thank you for your advice. It was most helpful,' I gushed, simply glad to have circumvented further interminable interrogation. Just as I was about to make myself scarce, Demelza launched back into her tortuous tale, with Piedmont pacing back and forth on his curlicued pediment: 'Well, that wasn't the denouement of our epic tragedy! Having heroically fended off our imbecilic intimidators, frenetic gunfire suddenly began to reverberate around the bosky valley basin. We espied the tweeded sable-haired seigneur of the château below us as we glided on the estival zephyrs. Apoplectic with rage, he showered us with an incensed salvo of shots. Valentino was faltering, his arthritic wing giving him gyp. We exhorted him to soar higher, we endeavoured to spur him on, but... but...'

'Mercy! Enough is enough! My shattered soul cannot abide this savagery! Alas and alack, my venerated confrère Valentino has shuffled off this mortal coil!' lamented a distraught Piedmont, his ululating cry piercing my steaming ears. 'Our blithesome undergraduate days will forever be imprinted on my fragile mind!'

Hugo's tyrannical throttlehold of the valley was tightening. And what was this unhealthy obsession with blasting everything to smithereens? Demelza flittered off to console her hysterical husband, tenderly preening his ruffled feathers.

'I'm so sorry for your loss,' I sympathised, attempting to not sound trite. For me, well-meant platitudes had been little more than painful prompts to grieve. I now appreciated just how difficult it was to know what to say.

'Wheeding and keeyodeling have carried us through our mournful melancholia,' explained a sanguine Demelza. The consolatory contours of the curative Washwell were assuaging their anguish too.

'Pardon my ignorance, but what's keeyodeling?' I probed inquisitively. My vocabulary was certainly expanding with each day spent in this bountiful valley.

'Let us show you,' suggested a now-perkier Piedmont, flapping up to the topmost polished marble frieze with his lettered ally close behind.

As I watched them taking wing into the healing hope-filled Washwell, I regretted misjudging these hovering books. Whilst their academic arrogance was exasperating, they were far more sensitive than I'd first realised. Whether great or small, and with all their complicated problems and eccentricities, each and every creature deserved a voice. Not least Mum.

If I could just persuade her to accompany me on my adventure tomorrow! At one with the uplifting undulations of the valley, Mum's faith in the world might be restored. Hopefully she wouldn't need too much convincing. She'd jump at the chance of a walk, and with the progress of the last week perhaps she'd even be up for some natural nourishment too.

In any case, observing the broken-hearted brainboxes wheeling and diving on the thermals, I acknowledged that even if you could fly, healing took time.

The scintillating morning sunshine illuminated the pearly fanned tail feathers of the plumed polymaths. From below, their intricate ivory-stippled undersides were a startling contrast to their drab jackets. The restorative power of the lush landscape was palpable. As the glisten-bespeckled buzzards circled effortlessly on the breeze overhead, the heaving hillside echoed their relief.

Keeyodeling was seemingly a hybrid of buteonine ballet and opera. Drifting ethereally between graceful cabrioles and crescendoing 'kee-ows', bold bravuras and bel canto cries, these culture vultures were in their element. With their kee-owing cabaletta resounding in my enraptured ears, I felt it was time to leave these comforted connoisseurs to their wild Washwell enlightenment. My warm farewell wave was answered with a mewing fortissimo 'adieu' as I sauntered back to Trolliloes in a rather reflective mood.

Re-energised by a perfect picnic in Dad's fern-fringed beech bower, my eager ears were crying out for another countryside caper. Doubling back on myself, I opted to explore a different stretch of the fluorite, filigree forest. With distant 'kee-ows' still ringing around the whispering Washwell, I'd hopefully be treated to a harmonious finale from the flawless falcon on my homeward journey.

Popcorn putters were bursting in my expectant ear canals as I ambled along the flexuous figwort-lined footpath. My brain was still throbbing from its highbrow gymnastics and the sylvan sanctum provided a head-calming cooldown. A whirling wood white butterfly led me further along the rutted root-knobbled track. The sweet flutey warble of a nasal whitethroat was a soothing soundtrack to my enchanted exploration.

All of a sudden, a faint rustling within the fronded jungle gave way to the sound of an animated voice: 'On your marks, get set, skittingle!'

A nimble creature bounded in from my left, trampling the chartreuse carpet in its wake. Leaping lithely over the pathway like a champion cervine hurdler came a dynamic chestnut doe. As she sprang off pell-mell into the umber tangle, her moonstone-mottled coat glimmered in the shafts of iridescent sunlight seeping through the knotted canopy. Hot on her hooves galloped a freckled bronze buck, vaulting deftly over the track and off into the spangled woodland weave.

'Beat you! Beat you! Ner ner ner ner ner! You can't outskittingle Orion!' hollered the taunting hind from somewhere amongst the wooded wilderness.

'Wanna bet? I reckon that minutes can be shaven off my personal best today! You'd better up your galloping game, sister!' jeered the boastful buck, allowing himself an unsporting head start and thus inciting the clear indignation of his fleet-hooved female foe.

Faster than I could say Buck Robinson, the macho male whipped over the long jump pit-path like a whirlwind. Seconds later, his equally competitive rival rollicked by, whining that her challenger's cheating tactics were 'below the pelt'. These acrobatic athletes gambolled zippily off towards their fallen-oak finish line, with the melanistic male providing a cocky self-congratulatory commentary. For a moment it looked like it would be a dead heat, but the bragging buck eventually managed to romp triumphantly home, much to the annoyance of his whingeing adversary.

'He came, he saw, he conquered! With all the graceful prowess of Kris Akabosky, the stellar skittingle title holder strikes again! Whoop whoop!' vaunted the vain victor, rubbing the disgruntled doe's snout in it.

'Aargh! Stop being such a blithering big fawn, Alby! You really are the limit! Just you wait, my infuriating friend; I'll show you in the decider! Top doe Orion will reign supreme again!' goaded a peeved similarly puerile Orion, pawing at the moss-carpeted clay in a fit of pique. 'None of your underhand stunts, mind you, Mr. Trumpet-Blower.'

It felt like I was piggy in the middle of this petty deer domestic. A baritone bellow from the cocoa-coloured buck signalled the final lap, and then they were off! Their self-centred cervine fanfaronade didn't endear me to either of the lithe contenders. Darting through the dense undergrowth with steely-eyed determination, I wondered whether they'd even notice me?

'Whoa! Hang on a minute there, Ori!' whispered the wary buck, grinding to an abrupt standstill. 'Look, there's an invader on the track up ahead!'

Frozen to the spot, they both eyed me up carefully from the security of their dappled camouflaged covert.

'Aww, but look, she's got a kind face, and I just *love* her chic blue pelt – check out those stripes! And what's that funky rainbow growth on her rump?' shrieked a fidgety Orion, unable to contain her excitement. 'On balance, I think we should dip our dewclaws in, Alby. If you obey all the rules, you miss all of the fun. You never know, she might be able to give me some fashion tips!'

Hushed murmurs ensued as they chewed their comfrey-cud and assessed the potential threat. I'd always considered deer to be such skittish creatures, but these bold gymnasts seemed keen to embrace everything. Their cut-throat cervine contest abandoned, they edged suspiciously towards me through the bracken shin-tangle. Even so, they chose to remain at the golden hypericum-hemmed path's edge in order to test the water.

'I *adore* your glossy bellflower-blue fur. What's your secret, if you don't mind me asking?' exclaimed the style-conscious spotted doe. 'I'm Orion, by the way. Pleased to meet you.'

It was rather ironic that I'd always gone out of my way to *not* be in vogue, preferring instead to choose an outfit which was practical and vaguely clean. Life was too short to agonise over modish trends when you could be making a difference in the world. I'd take the compliment, though.

'Hi there! I'm Ella. Lovely to meet you both. Well, I think your conker-coloured coat sets off your fern-tinted eyes beautifully,' I ventured, hoping that some flagrant flattery might detract from my patent lack of flair.

'And I'm Albemarle. Glorious afternoon, isn't it? Do excuse my sister. It was only this morning that I was dragged up to the meadow mall for another interminable hoofbling expedition! Just how many pairs of scabious stilettos does a doe need, for goodness' sake?' bemoaned the down-to-earth buck.

I was just incredulous that deer accessorised their hooves with wildflower 'shoes'!

'Oi, you! Those purple selfheal-sandals will see me through the rest of the season, thank you very much. Besides, got to get myself in tip-top condition for the rut if I'm to have any chance of meeting a tall, dark stranger,' explained the defensive doe, eager to justify her materialistic instinct.

Munching through the wooded thicket like there was no tomorrow, these furred foodies were clearly fans of the finer things in life. The esurient epicures eulogised the wild angelica amuse-bouche, raved about the mouth-watering marjoram and sang the praises of the delectable dead-nettle dessert. Oh, how I hungered for Mum and me to rediscover such a carefree relationship with food!

'Grab life by the antlers! That's our motto in life. Nine years on this earth, and that's if we're lucky. Better make them pretty darn amazing, that's what I say!' implored the gregarious male gourmand, chewing on a sprig of coralroot.

'We love this time of year! Pinecone tennis season, you see. Nothing beats a cloudless day spent watching a gripping game and sipping an ice-cold elderberry cordial. Today's the day of the grand finale – John McEndoe versus Boris Bucker on Centre Field. I expect deer have been camping in the queue for days, but we're hoping for a spot on McEndoe Mound. Do you fancy tagging along?' asked a sparky Orion, jiggling about in anticipation of the big match. Her boisterous brother was equally exhilarated, whirling around the brushwood like a stag with four antlers.

'Ooh, yes, please! Sounds like we'll have a ball!' I enthused, bouncing up and down at the idea of this surreal cervine Wimbledon. From beautifying badgers to balletic buzzards, I thought I'd seen it all, but my reawakening senses just kept going from strength to bizarre strength.

'Well, we'd better get a hoof on then! Will the McEndoe dynamo win the Grand Slam? Let's skittingle, I can barely contain myself!' whooped an amped Albemarle, already sprinting off like the deuce down the zig-zagging footpath.

Coming to the conclusion that when in the Washwell it was best to do as the Washwellites did, I allowed myself to charge through the kaleidoscopic ravel with all the merry abandon of my pelting playfellows. Bounding over sun-baked ditches, tearing through groves of towering goatsbeard and hurtling around lichen-plated tree stumps, we weaved through the luminous, bewitching woodland, our gleeful gales of laughter howling through the secluded sanctuary. With blood coursing through my invigorated veins, I was alive once more!

Clearing a storm-toppled beech tree with a frisky curvet, we frolicked towards a ramshackle stile which led to a murmuring meadow. Dad and I had never managed to fulfil our Wimbledon dream, but now I'd made it to the hallowed turf of Centre Court, or at least the deer version thereof.

Jostling through the throng of cervine spectators, we helped ourselves to bark bowlfuls of blackberries and elderflower cream and desperately scoured the heaving hill for a spot to enjoy the action. Eventually ensconced amongst a lively lek of bachelor bucks, I absorbed every diverting detail of this sporting spectacle. There was a bevy of cone fawns poised to ensure the smooth running of the championship, an austere-looking umpire perched on his molehill chair and a sprinkling of cervine celebrities, including – much to a swooning Orion's delight – the archstag of Sussex!

The electrified herd immediately hushed down at the emergence of two swaggering leucistic stags from the shaded sycamore sideline. After much portentous parading and conceited chest-thumping, they limbered up at opposite ends of the twig-defined court for the much-anticipated clash.

More on the ball than I was with this farcical fixture, Albemarle helpfully pointed out which challenger was which. A frisky freckled fawn tossed a pinecone between the swollen-headed stags and they shot post haste towards it, each issuing stentorian grunts that Rafael Nadal himself would have been proud of. Catching the pine shuttlecock with his velveted antlers, a puffed-up Bucker hurled it back to his restless opponent with a forceful forehorn. An accomplished ping-pong volley ensued, the cone being propelled expertly back and forth between the bitter rivals. Breathtaking backhorn flings were answered by lusty lightning lobs as the twinkle-hooved superstars jigged around the makeshift court.

But the exuberant oohs and aahs of the fired-up audience were instantly silenced by the thunderous rumble of two vehicles barrelling breakneck towards the big match. Hysterical hinds, intimidated bucks and frantic fawns all suddenly skedaddled helter-skelter into their beech-sheltered bolthole, leaving me marooned on the deserted mound.

I sat a moment to spy on the strident speeding invaders, until I discovered that the maniacal driver of the gleaming ebony Chelsea tractor was none other than brutish Bellington-Fraser himself! At this, I scurried lickety-split into the welcoming woodland, as spooked as my cervine companions by the ignoble intruder.

Crouching behind a rambling snarl of black bindweed, I took stock of the scene unfolding before my binoculars. Hugo was now striding around the field gesticulating to a portly ruddy-faced man who could barely keep up with the domineering bully. They paced around the grass taking measurements and did a perfunctory recce of the fencing and gates. After a final vehement exchange and a vice-like handshake, they careered off at full tilt just as heedlessly as they'd bombed in. It was then that I was able to decipher the slogan on the tailgate of the obsequious aide's Land Rover:

*Bungehurst Farm Venison*
*Award-winning, prime quality farmed deer*
*from the heart of Sussex*

It seemed that Hugo was now after a finger in this juicy profit-making pie as well. Hell-bent on clipping the wings of each and every Washwellite, his mercenary monopolisation of the valley was cranking up.

The infuriating injustice of this abject state of affairs was enough to send my magpie nemesis into a flailing frenzy. As it thrashed around wildly in my inflamed mind, it suddenly dawned that the ball was now in *my* court to thwart this dastardly villain. For the sake of every single creature I'd had the pleasure of meeting, and as payback for Dad's maltreatment, I racked my battered brain for a fitting vengeance.

After a meditative meander through the shock absorbing boscage of Trolliloes, the ultimate retribution was now staring me in the face! A prominent poster plastered to the rusting kissing gate reminded me of the upcoming game and country fair. With all the tempestuous trials and tribulations of the past fortnight, I'd completely forgotten about this theatrical Hugo-fest. It was imperative that I found a way of hampering this flashy ego-trip! I had to spike this noxious narcissist's guns! Pushing through the creaky gate, my buzzing mind began to grind into action.

As I hatched my guileful game plan, I glanced over at Bellington-Fraser's nauseating neoclassical eyesore. But what was the indistinct avian form sprawled lifeless at the foot of the marble monstrosity? I dashed frenetically towards it with dazzling pied flashes smarting my enraged eyes and prickles of panic pulsing through my shuddering body. In a petrified piebald fluster, I woefully confronted Hugo's ghastly coup de grâce. For there, lying listless on the grandiose plinth, with a gaping gunshot wound to its wing and terror glinting in its obsidian eyes, was the silent peregrine.

CHAPTER 9

# NINE FOR A KISS

How I'd managed to convey the frail motionless peregrine all the way from the abhorrent arch back to the safe emerald embrace of Heartsease, I'll never know.

Just when I'd thought that the handsome hematite tercel had kissed the dust, it had cocked its velvety head up at me and issued a silent cri de cœur from its anguished opalescent eyes. The forlorn falcon had, however, been extraordinarily lucky. Whilst it was clearly in a state of shock, on closer inspection the blood-caked battle scar had luckily been a mere glancing blow. If this heinous offence had been a Bellington-Fraser special, then it was a blessing that he was such a poor shot.

But it had been painfully evident that the poor sublime soul needed to be nursed back to full health. With the whole valley being forced to dance to Hugo's harsh tune, it had felt as if *I* was the only person capable of protecting this unwanted ermine-robed wretch. And so I'd tenderly wrapped the stunned, compliant victim in my leavers' hoodie for our homeward peregrination, hoping that Mum and I would be able to kiss away its suffering.

Cradling its delicate Prussian blue plumage in my trembling hands, we'd trekked down the steep descent, tiptoed tensely past the incompetent sniper's narcissistic château and trudged wearily back up to the consoling sage-green refuge. Pied cackles had pealed in my overtaxed ears as I'd latched the yew-canopied gate. With all the pre-aisle jitters of our silver-frocked sylvan bride, I'd apprehensively ascended to our little shrine, a descant of persuasive defence resounding in my flustered head.

Uncertain whether I could butter fat-phobic Mum up, I'd known for sure that I daren't mention Mr. big gun Bellington-Fraser. Reference to Dad's nefarious whipcracking ringmaster risked a disastrous topple from her precarious tightrope-walk recovery. Fondling my blood-stained falconine bouquet, I'd spied Mum through the kitchen window, her arms seemingly entangled in an elaborate yoga asana. Just relieved that it wasn't the previous week's corpse pose, I'd skulked timidly up to the back door with piebald pins and needles pricking at my clammy skin.

Half expecting to find Mum in the throes of a strenuous sun salutation, I'd been heartened to find her wrestling with the stand mixer and dusted in icing sugar. The crimson KitchenAid had been Dad's final extravagant Christmas present to her. Whilst not a star baker, Mum had previously enjoyed rustling up a crunchy ginger biscuit here and a sticky pineapple upside-down cake there. But since the acrid catastrophe of Dad's death, the impressive mixer had only gathered an ever-thicker layer of dust in the corner of the flat's galley kitchen.

Sauntering in with my shocked avian offering had been unhelpful startling interference midway through her pavlova preparations. However, after a lengthy piercing Hollywood glare and some sweet-talk from her former chief spoon-licker, it had been *my* turn to be astounded. Swirling the glossy meringue mixture into rugged peaks, she'd calmly detailed the equipment we'd need to save this 'poor scrap'. Bewildered by Mum's pragmatism, I was bathed in elation as showers of shimmering sunlight confetti twirled at my fatigued feet.

Since when had Mum moonlighted as a veterinary nurse? Was this a glimpse of the kind-hearted 'a kiss will make it better' spirit of my childhood? If only she could show herself this much compassion! After the traumatic loss of her even-the-burnt-bits biscuit taster, her canine scourge had relentlessly been reining the 'real Mum' in. And I'd despaired of ever seeing my loving life-grabbing ally again.

Nestled in Dad's snuggly teal beanbag with our mutilated inpatient on my lap, Mum's sedating sobs had reverberated around the treatment room. Our wounded warrior seemed to be listening just as intently as I was as she'd launched into her touching explanatory story. Clag-caked and sodden from their downland footslog, Mum and Dad had once saved an injured robin and nursed it back to health together. With Mum on feeding duties and Dad on crooked wing care, they'd made the perfect animal rescue team.

The showstopper dessert now in the oven, Mum had hurriedly gathered together our vet's bag of improvised apparatus. Using her cake tester as a surgeon's scalpel, she'd delicately pierced breathing holes in the sides of a packing box and then diligently lined it with Dad's old succour-infused dressing-gown. Darting to her newly baptised baking cupboard, she'd pulled out the icing syringe we'd used to decorate my stunning tenth birthday tiger cake.

Using the dregs of her Silver Spoon to concoct a sugar solution, we'd retired to the sofa for our plumed patient's welcome meal. As we'd watched the seemingly ravenous peregrine taking its first sweet sips, there were fond recollections of choice avian encounters with our ardent birdwatching champion. For me it was a mesmerising buff and ivory bespeckled barn owl. And Mum's dewy-eyed memory was of a glossy bronze-stippled cormorant on a sandy Devon shore.

After benevolently bathing the laceration in salt water, we'd retreated to the tranquil sanctuary of the spare room and gently placed the sated convalescent in its packing box pen. Our desecrated wreck salvaged from the brink, bowlfuls of craggy raspberry-wreathed scrumptiousness had been our mouth-watering reward.

Two blissful lasagne-fuelled days had followed, with Mum playing dedicated head vet and me as her dependable auxiliary. Through exhausting four hourly feeds of warmed raw chicken to assiduous gash cleansing, we'd proved the ultimate raptor rescue squad. As the now fulgent-eyed falcon had become increasingly restless, my other poorly soldier had started to spread her weakened wings too. When not juggling our strict drumstick regimen, we'd sowed some sunflower seeds to brighten up the patio, cuddled up to watch *Chocolat* whilst polishing off our own box of Black Magic and French-plaited each other's hair, all accompanied by the giggly gabber of yore.

Fretting that the velvet-caped invalid's wings would waste away, Mum had sent me into the garden in search of a practice runway. After exhuming the previous owners' splintery rabbit run from a sprawling camouflage of conifers, we'd set it up under the twinkle-mottled shelter of Dad's lime oak awning. With the addition of a regal log throne, cosy cardboard hunting lodge and water parterre, the princely peregrine palace was ready! Seemingly enraptured by its sumptuous mansion, the majestic hematite-robed monarch had tentatively fluttered its Prussian blue pinion in gratification. The mangled wing was visibly on the mend and now my other airsick nestling needed help to fly.

The Washwell Valley had become so much a part of me that I ached for Mum to join me in its Gaian arms. Over a serene quarrel-free lunch on the following day, Mum had immediately agreed to an afternoon foray into its nurturing contours. For the moment I decided to keep my auditory superpower quiet, still fearing that my new-found effusive friends were merely a magpie-induced mirage. Besides, a dose of Piedmont, Orion and Frau Strumpwaffle might overly complicate our adventure.

After a brief check on our exalted patient, I waited under the sapphire-streaked Mr. Whippy sky for my ice cream-loving pal to emerge. The front flowerbed was now embellished with a fragrant gilded rosebush, sprinkled in reams of xanthic blousy blossoms. Flaunting its intricate attire to the gleaming valley, the cinnabar-encrusted lacquerware fan of a red admiral butterfly graced the purple-panicled buddleia.

And then came Mum, without a canine fandangle in sight, her Titian tresses tumbling about her raw-boned shoulders. Wearing a scarlet Bardot top accessorised with spotted silk scarf and Breton tote bag, she looked effortlessly chic. A lick of smoky mascara accentuated her polished mahogany eyes and her preppy cropped jeans were now not nearly as roomy. Whilst not classic rambling apparel, I was overjoyed that the graceless greyhound wasn't dictating an outmoded trend and forcing her into the dreaded repressive gym gear.

The August day had been sultry enough since first light, and now, with the sun just crossing its roasting zenith, the whole of the Washwell glistened with iridescent heat. After a boosting and for once not brushed-off hug, we strode forth arm in arm into the billowy green ocean.

Entering Flitterbrook Lane, Mum started up the parched track, as if her insatiable canine, hungry for another hearty course of arduous aerobics, had awoken from its momentary slumber and was now tugging at its leash.

Taking my novice intrepid explorer by the hand, I gently guided her towards the aqueduct of arched oak guardians. I sensed a little resistance in her shoestring French fry fingers, perhaps the tension of a conflicted soul, but as we were enticed further into the divine glinting dale, Mum's shoulders noticeably relaxed and she murmured, 'It's beautiful. Just like those lush Devon combes we used to explore.' With a tear trickling down her sniffling nose, she continued, 'Dad giving you a piggyback and me breathing in the honeysuckle and ozone.'

'He was really on to something with Heartsease, wasn't he?' I suggested, giving her bony hand a sympathetic squeeze.

As a torrent of tranquillising tears erupted onto the elephant-skin earth beneath our itchy feet, I tried to cling on to a positive vibe: 'Well, for his sake, let's go and enjoy it! There's so much to see, Mum, it's glorious!'

After another bolstering bear hug and administration of a tissue from my six-months-of-solid-sobbing stockpile, we ambled down the beech-cushioned calm of the sunken track. Outstretched ivory tassels of shepherd's purse offered their condolences and the azure glister of a dragonfly lured us deeper into the analeptic Eden.

Clambering over the gate, Bellington-Fraser's egomaniacal motif glowered irately back at us. But jumping down into the chicory-stippled powder blue patchwork beyond, I noticed a subtle change to the chains. Although still protecting Hugo's utopian principality, the rusted tangle now hung loosely and the thick moss armour had been removed. Someone must have unlocked it, if only for a moment. Hopefully this was a serendipitous sign that Mum's own degenerate jailer was finally slackening its stranglehold.

Meandering through the speedwell-embroidered eiderdown, Mum abruptly halted, her enthralled eyes gazing skyward. She squinted into the glaring sun and promptly cradled my appreciative 'I'm hurting too' hand. Descending like a mellifluous heaven-sent marionette, floated a sonorous skylark, its jubilant exaltation thronging the heady air. Mum's eyes closed, twitching with dreamy memory at this enchanting miniature virtuoso. Captivated by the celestial soloist, we stood for ten harmonious minutes, hands entwined, in silent reverence.

'It's the night-time that's worst,' Mum uttered gloomily, despondent at her less romantic reality. 'For most of the day I can just about cope, but in bed, *our* bed, the bed we bought the day after we came back from honeymoon…' she faltered, the spring of resentment welling up once more.

'It still smells of Dad, you know. When the lights are out, I feel as if I can just reach across and touch him. Sometimes I try, as if it really was all a bad dream. But he's not here, he'll never be here, and I just can't forgive myself.'

Threading our way through the virescent voile of Giffords Wood, Mum unburdened her lamentful load with each soothing step. Pearly racemes of enchanter's nightshade fringed our peaceful passage to the moonstone glimmer of the Washwell below. Now a sinuous summer trickle, we paused on the footbridge to contemplate the kaleidoscopic quiet.

A spate of sorrow now streaming down her prominent cheekbones, Mum whimpered, 'I knew he was deeply unhappy, knew for years. I could have done something, Ella, told him to stop at Capstone. I could see it all and I did nothing! I even encouraged him to stay until we'd moved to Heartsease. "Wait until the mortgage has cleared," I said – like a bloody bank manager!'

The true nature of Mum's guileful greyhound had finally become crystal clear – it was her overwhelming guilt. For six months she had silently schlepped it around, and day by day it had consumed her. The endless exercise was her attempt at escape, the piffling portions her penance for the wrong she could not right.

As the sun-baked brook was filled anew with Mum's penitent grief, I pondered on what I'd learnt from the animals. Wilf and Wilbur's simple acceptance of life's transience, the gold that illuminated even the darkest corners of Hilaire and Colette's joydle, and lastly, Piedmont and Demelza soaring above their feathered and feather-blasting foes.

'Mum,' I croaked, stroking her bone-weary, hound-hammered body, 'Dad loved you more than anything in the world. He never would have wanted you to blame yourself for what happened.'

'But I… I should have stopped it…' she sobbed, fiddling with the silver skylark pendant in anguish.

'You loved and cared for him more than anyone else in the world, *you* encouraged him to follow his dream and buy Heartsease. What would Dad say if he saw us now?' I asked, fondling Mum's quivering hands and staring empathetically into her frantic fawn's eyes.

'He would have told me to stop being so silly and get on with exploring the world,' she gulped, the hint of a smile creasing across her haggard face. 'He once said, when I found out your granddad had passed away, "The journey never really ends, even if we have to walk a different path."'

With knowing grins spreading across our flushed faces, we held each other close and bawled into the beatific, brindled serenity. Dad always had an uncanny knack for finding the right words.

A jaunty dunnock's piped farewell fanfare serenaded us as we left the cool cocoon of the dappled woodland weave and began our climb to the stallionback field. Mum seemed a little brighter, as if some of the woes of the past months had been washed downstream. We imagined what Dad would have made of Hugo's pustulous pleasure palazzo as I hurried Mum past its gaudy gates. Through stippled sweet chestnut arcades, past swathes of aureate celandine and along wild strawberry-hemmed hedgerows, we scaled the steep-sided ridge with more chatter than ever before.

After Mum's initial goggle-eyed reaction to the heinous Arc de Hugo: 'Whoever built it must have had a taste-bypass at birth!', we sat at its frigid marble foot to admire the verdant sweeping whale's back breaching on the other side of the valley. Swaddled in the sea-green surf, we were swept away in its splendour. Breakers of ivory eyebright winked at us and drifts of coral-studded vetch crowns rippled in the soft breeze.

After our swell immersion, Mum fumbled in her striped Mary Poppins bag and retrieved a faded brown envelope. Handing it to me, I pulled out a pot-pourri of old photographs. As I leafed through them, my own salty spindrift was churned up. With tears gushing down my cheeks, I perused this nostalgic treasure trove. Amongst others, there was me on Dad's lap excitedly anticipating a choppy ferry ride to Brownsea Island, Mum and me on the funicular ascending the Zugspitze, and Dad gazing awestruck into my rosy, crinkled face on the day I was born. Eventually, I happened upon a dog-eared sepia-tinged snap, a veritable catalogue of '80s fashion faux pas. Perched on the bough of a gnarled tree was a lanky, bespectacled boy, and beside him a tanned, avuncular man sporting a broad grin.

'Who's that?' I enquired, trying to place where I'd seen the man's familiar weathered face before.

'Well, the little boy is obviously Dad – his taste in glasses barely changed,' joked Mum, fingering the bleached picture. 'But I've no idea who this fellow is. It's the earliest photo of Dad I could find – you know Nana still has all his baby photos!'

I studied the print more closely, cudgelling my throbbing brain to identify the genial gentleman. And then, like a lucent wintry morning, it suddenly dawned on me – Dad's kindly custodian was none other than Mungo Dunthorpe!

'Mungo?!' I breathed.

'What was that, darling?' asked Mum absent-mindedly, tenderly caressing a shot of us at the real Arc de Triomphe.

'Nothing, Mum,' I swiftly retorted. The last thing I wanted was to alert her to Hugo's presence in the valley. 'Hey, do you want to try something fun?'

Ushering Mum to the sweltering crest of the swirling sward ocean, my racing mind was swooping like a predatory peregrine. How did Dad know Mungo? Why didn't he recall coming here? Would Mungo remember Dad? I resolved to quiz Hugo's hapless, limping lackey the next time our paths crossed.

'Now, a good friend once told me that when life's getting you down, just charge down a hill!' I explained as we conquered the searing summit. Prickleballing Wilf and Wilbur-style wasn't really an option with Mum's painfully protruding ribs – I didn't want to have two bruised birds to worry about.

Perhaps it was the prospect of a more taxing workout, or maybe a genuine desire to bathe in the beauty of the Washwell, but joyously Mum wholeheartedly agreed to this frivolity. Fussing that her hair would get in her face, she insisted on shackling it with the vile, restrictive headband before we took the revitalising plunge.

'Ready, steady, *go!*' I shouted, and we hurtled down the hillside, canine-imposed inhibitions being flung off left, right and centre. The foul fettering hairband was promptly whisked away by the frolicsome wind, granting Mum's lustrous locks their liberty once more.

'Wooohoooo,' shrieked Mum, her auburn ringlets sparkling in the brilliant afternoon sunshine. 'This is *such* fun!'

Three more times we galloped down the heaving hill, each time more exhilarating than the last, my mum resuscitated before my gladdened eyes. The curative contours had administered their kiss of life and now my rekindled companion gave me a doting peck, nuzzling me closer than her affection-phobic pooch had ever permitted. After months of canine cold-shouldering, now here we were hugging and kissing like… well, like mother and daughter.

Fizzing with euphoria, I had intended to take the same route home, but a pair of ugly dark smears in the distance forced me to reconsider. It was the unmistakeable hulk of Hugo and his Wilf-worrying hellhound. The despicable duo were swaggering up from Socknersh like a couple of hooligans. I was certain Mum would recognise Hugo and couldn't risk anything setting back her recovery. So I hastily diverted us towards the tumbledown safety of Glydwish Farm, leaving Mr. Beastly Face and his repulsive sidekick to their roguery.

Retrieving Mum's trusty tote bag, we descended the sighing milkwort-duned meadow, as if it too were reluctant to part company. My magpie menace had been refreshingly absent for the whole expedition, and enveloped in the valley's oceanic undulations, with mum returning to something of her old self, I sensed a sunset to our sadness.

Our arrival at Heartsease was announced as grandly as the entrance to any society dinner by the strident call to arms of our noble falcon. The tumultuous chirring of a spirited grasshopper fêted our appearance as we were shepherded under the cerise sequined Chinese bean tree by a zealous amber-jewelled painted lady butterfly.

Reaching our recuperating royalty, we were cheered to find it scooting around its lavish estate, the whirr of its wings almost lifting the bulky cage. The rallying raptor was now utterly transformed from the pitiful waif I had rescued. With a sharp pang of sadness stabbing at my heart, I reluctantly agreed that the time was right to release our blessed bird. Still, I would forever cherish these rewarding past few days spent with my other formidable fighter.

Mum volunteered to fetch a final supper for the glitter-eyed tercel to boost its flight to freedom. I waited expectantly beside its stately enclosure like a proud parent at their child's graduation, cameraphone in hand, ready to capture the gleeful celebration.

But as the clock ticked, agonising disquiet gnawed away at me. Where had Mum got to? Surely it didn't take that long to find some goodbye chicken canapés? Horrifyingly, the answer became apparent as she burst from the house in a frenzied mascara-smudged flood of tears. Brandishing a letter in her hand, she stormed towards me, her distressed howls drowning out our keyed-up convalescent's cry.

Scanning the venomous missive, I was instantly alarmed by the letterhead's belligerent black-and-white blemish. Taunting my flustered eyes was the inane masonry-based logo of Capstone Consulting!

*Dear Mrs. Pearson,*

*It has come to our attention that you are **still** in possession of a Capstone Consulting laptop despite a full six months having passed since Andy Pearson abruptly terminated his service to the company.*

*Given the excessive and entirely unjustified time that has passed since the said termination of said service, we now consider your actions in retaining said laptop amount to **theft** and have instructed our lawyers – Welldriss, Smythewick and Hardon LLP – to act accordingly.*

*Please note, unless the laptop is **immediately** returned, our lawyers will be taking the matter further with the police.*

*Yours sincerely,*

*Maxine Skelthorne*

*Executive Director of Human Capital Assets, Capstone Consulting*

*cc Algernon Smythewick, Managing Partner, Welldriss, Smythewick and Hardon LLP*

*cc Hugo Bellington-Fraser, Chief Executive Officer, Capstone Consulting*

Like an ominous death knell, my maleficent magpie's derisive sniggers echoed in my fuming ears. Pelting me with a salvo of piebald pecks, it jeered at my earlier misplaced hope. Why hadn't I offered to go inside to get the snack? I could have dealt with the poisonous post without tormenting my frail little skylark! With Mum threatening to don her démodé gym kit for a penitent pounding of the garden, I feared we were kissing goodbye to her fledgling recovery.

CHAPTER 10

# TEN FOR A SURPRISE
# YOU MUST NOT MISS

I cannot recall a more torturous, fury-triggered fit of insomnia than that which followed the Capstone summons. The stomach-churning dispatch had set Mum's ravenous greyhound growling with renewed gusto. After lengthy cajoling, I'd eventually convinced her that supper was preferable to self-flagellation; even so, her appetite, so strong in the past few days, had virtually vanished. Limbering up for our macaroni marathon, I'd painfully watched her silently prodding at the mountainous maggot's nest, tonight's finish line an endurance test too far. As she'd sloped zombie-like off to bed, I'd despaired of her ever building up the stamina to recover.

Like an exasperating earworm, my malicious magpie's taunting cackles had run on loop through my restless mind. Daybreak's blood-spattered butcher's apron sky was a grim reminder that Hugo was, quite literally, calling the shots in the valley. Having attempted to assassinate the Washwell's majestic sparkle-eyed sovereign, the Slaughterman of Socknersh was now hell-bent on ripping out Mum's entrails. How dare this brutish bully be so insensitive to my heartsick little skylark! Still peckish for some cervine silverside and leporine tenderloin, this murderous maniac was now whetting his cleaver's blade for a climactic, barbarous bloodbath. I urgently had to topple this merciless tyrant, before a chop-happy tragedy occurred!

In the fitful demi-dream which followed, I imagined exposing Mr. Bellington-Flesher for his crimes against nature. Overseeing courtroom proceedings was an implacable Piedmont Buteo, theatrically dressed in resplendent ostrich-feather wig and lavish gold taffeta gown, the jury comprising a motley hotchpotch of Orion, Hilaire, Suki, Wilbur and the august falcon. Just as the animals came to sentencing a whimpering Hugo, a piebald police force swooped down and snatched him away, dumping the remorseless miscreant before a fox firing squad.

Woken by a pied paroxysm of panic, I was confronted with the harsh reality of matters. Whilst I was sure that shooting raptors, baiting badgers and coursing carefree bunnies were offences, what was my concrete evidence? A human judge would hardly accept a rabbiting Wilf and Wilbur as credible witnesses for the prosecution!

The egocentric spectacle of the game fair loomed in my apoplectic pirouetting head. This was my chance to humiliate the hubristic self-proclaimed superstar! Ignoring the occasional sceptical peck from my corvine scourge, a sketchy stratagem hatched in my mind. I would certainly be returning Dad's life-draining laptop, but not quite in its previous grindstone guise. Musing on how my animal allies might disrupt proceedings, I now simply needed to convince them to help…

Visions of my vengeful game plan were abruptly interrupted by my rumbling tummy, keen for breakfast after last night's hunger-suppressing pasta hoo-ha. Dawn's fine-shred sky was now a bitter marmalade swirl, daubed atop the croissant-like contours of the valley. Creeping from my bedroom in search of revenge-fuelling victuals, I heard a faint creak coming from the kitchen. Who could this be so early in the morning – ravenous rodent or brazen burglar? The nectarean scent of raspberry conserve wafted into the living room and I was overjoyed to discover a furtive Mum slathering a pair of toasted crumpets with not only jam, but butter too!

'Oh, Mum!' I cried in relief, unable to contain my sleep-deprived emotions as I melted into her warm, buttery embrace.

'Ella, my love. I'm so sorry about last night,' Mum apologised, squeezing me close and stroking my tousled, throbbing bedhead with her sticky, soothing hands. 'That disgraceful letter just brought it all back. I was *so* upset and angry, I just didn't know where to put myself. I've been awake for hours, listening to my stomach grinding away. Would you like some crumpets?'

After the previous evening's dispiriting false start, our first-class breakfast of champions more than made up for it. With sleeping greyhounds left to lie, we must have devoured the full baker's dozen, Lurpak-scrumptiousness included. Full of toasted perfection, a chipper Mum was definitely raring to go when I offered to take care of the laptop.

'Are you sure, sweetie?' she asked, speeding through the washing-up as if her vital spark had been restored.

'Positive, I'll make sure Capstone gets what they deserve.' I smirked, my Machiavellian manoeuvres taking shape in my effervescent head.

As she eyed me suspiciously, I decided to hastily divert attention towards our still-captive convalescent. Wrapped up in yesterday's harried brouhaha, we'd quite forgotten the release of our regal raptor.

With the peregrine's liberation on the honey-drenched horizon, I zipped excitedly through the drying-up, whilst Mum rustled up a chicken breast brunch for our esteemed patient.

After racing through a blissful panic-purging, headache-hushing shower, Mum amazed me for the second time that morning by asking, 'I know Dad bought a bird box for Heartsease, would you like us to put it up together?'

Hurriedly pulling on my denim shorts, my heart skipped another joyful beat as I exclaimed I would like nothing more.

The scorching August sun was just cresting the protective oak's emerald-encrusted crown as we paraded up the red clover carpet to greet our distinguished falconine guest. A rowdy scrum of rouge-cheeked chaffinches blithely bugled our arrival from their silver birch minstrels' gallery. The princely peregrine was certainly dressed for the occasion, dazzling once again in his hematite tux, ermine dress shirt and amber brogues, a faded smudge of ochre the only proof of Hugo's villainy.

As if to emphasise the razzmatazz of the ceremony, the celebrity tercel beat its Prussian blue pinions in an almighty flourish and uttered a thankful 'kak-kak-kak'. After Mum made a short speech, I was given the honour of anointing our obsidian-eyed leading light with its freedom. With the glistening sylvan spotlight on our salvatory superstar, we retreated a little and waited hand in hand for its big moment.

But our avian VIP seemed to have caught a bad case of stage fright and refused to budge, strutting around his stately enclosure as if to soak up the encouraging audience applause. Just when I thought we were destined for a no-show, it propelled its bespangled torso skywards. Shakily at first, but with growing confidence, it climbed above its lime-green launch pad, testing its velvety wings with every flap. For what seemed like an eon, it hung motionless above us, steeling its fans for the grand finale. Diving dramatically from high, it arced around the house in a spectacular encore, before powering off into the effulgent Washwell.

'The world is his to explore,' murmured Mum wistfully as we caught our last glorious glimpse of its scimitar-stiff wings uniting once more with the shimmering chartreuse sheath of the valley.

The next act was our memorial to Dad. With the consoling call of the falcon still ringing in my ears, I fetched the wooden bird box from my room. Lovingly cradling its furrowed, resilient frame as if it were my cherished idol himself, I was perplexed to find Mum at the oak, her palette and brushes in hand. Although no Monet, she had enjoyed dabbling in watercolours – Dad had kindly gifted our budding impressionist a portable easel for her fortieth birthday. Her charming seascape of Banthorpe Cove was now felicitously displayed above Mum and Dad's bed.

'I thought we could paint a special epitaph on the bird box,' Mum explained. 'Something to remember Dad by forever more.'

After brief contemplation, we both agreed that there was only one phrase which truly encapsulated our beloved wanderer:

*'The world is yours to explore'*
*Andy Pearson*
*1974–2019*

With Mum's delicate scarlet calligraphy adorning Dad's ornithological ornament, it was left to me to shimmy up the tree and hang our hope-filled masterpiece.

'It looks wonderful,' Mum called up. 'I think Dad would be very proud.'

Back on the ground, another not-shrugged-off-squeeze ensued as we drank in our hero's memory and recalled the claret-tailed red kite we'd spotted from our Scottish bothy. With Mum's insatiable canine at least temporarily muzzled, and my pied persecutor off pestering another angst-ridden soul, we were free to appreciate the alluring sun-stippled landscape together.

After our momentous morning, it was doubly heartening that Mum's appetite hadn't foundered following the carb-energising crumpets. Culinary creativity was rekindled before my delighted eyes as Mum concocted an inviting vegetable risotto from the fridge's odds and sods. Between creamy forkfuls of flavour, we discussed our artistic visions for Heartsease's horticultural blank canvas. Without a doubt, we had to plant some tulip bulbs this autumn – Dad's favourite flower would then be the star exhibit in our colourful spring display! After a restorative mug of milky tea, I enquired whether Mum wanted to join me on another ramble through paradise, but she declined, grinning that her painting passion had been refired by our nest box flirtation.

Leaving Mum setting up her treasured easel in our inspirational Eden, I marched forth into the khaki-clad contours of the Washwell. My cunning strategy was to enlist an animal army to overthrow hostile Hugo, or at least cause enough of a scuffle to quash the dastardly despot. My battle of persuasion would commence with my youngest cunicular recruits. I had also taken the liberty of snaffling the photograph of Dad and Mungo, and I yearned to cross paths with Field Marshal B-F's genial General to provide some Dad denouement.

Reaching the lustre-mottled tranquillity of Trolliloes, I remembered that Wilbur had mentioned they lived 'in elderberry warren near the crooked yew'. A bear hug of my leafy-locked comrade-in-arms kick-started my auditory superpower and thus my consentient soldier scout began. After our joggletailing japes, bobgazing frolics and the laugh-a-minute prickleballing caper, I was eagerly anticipating another delicious encounter with my chocolate button-eyed buddies.

Crossing a trail of industrious wood ants, I spied the tangled, contorted limbs of an ancient yew, resting its umber arms on a filigree futon of ivory bedstraw. Pausing expectantly, my sausage-sizzling ears listened out for the exuberant whoops and bellows of my rabbiting chums. But apart from the shrill hum of a loitering hoverfly, all was unnervingly silent.

Not wanting to be rude, I chose to wait for the playful pair to hop by, perching on a lichen-speckled stump to consider Dad's laptop. Closing my eyes, I pictured the self-centred screensaver, the imperious Chief Exploitative Officer at the bullseye with his farcical foundational pillar stones spiralling around his big head like a swarm of pesky bluebottles. Titanic Spirit indeed! Captain B-F was about to meet his iceberg, and with frosty spicules of rage flooding through my veins, I cooked up a recipe for retaliation. I would knock up a new, equally boastful background, this time eulogizing Dad and *his* qualities, and set it as the capstone to my Hugo-fest furore. Now all I needed was a troop of game guerrillas to complete the showboat-sinking chaos!

But where were the rollicking rascals? With a growing sense of unease I began hunting for the fabled warren. Perhaps it was teatime and Mr. Rabbit was preparing a toothsome nettle stew, or were the scampish couple savouring another game of prittleleaping? A passing buff-tailed bumblebee drew my gaze to a powder puff of snowy white caught on a snarl of bramble. The corvine thorn in my side spitefully chortled as I twigged that this was no blameless blowball but the wispy blood-flecked scut of a rabbit. With whirling flitterblossoms in my stomach, I called out in panic, 'Wilbur! Wilf! It's Ella, where are you?'

There was no response and, ducking knife-like piebald nips, I stumbled into the thistle-thick shin-tangle, scanning for the warren. Had the unthinkable happened? Was *that* what huntsman Hugo and his bunny-guzzling greyhound were up to last night?

My sweaty skin bristled in trepidation as I galloped frenetically through the dense underscrub. Cantering through a paddock of bracken, my boot caught and I tumbled onto a straggle of groundsel. Dusting myself down, I was ecstatic to discover that my assailant was a burrow at the foot of an imposing elder tree. This was my dynamic duo's welcoming digs!

I hollered down the hole until I was hoarse, frantic to find my frisky friends. My anguished cries were finally answered by a muted squeak: 'Miss Ella? Is that you?'

After protracted paw twisting, two quaking scraps emerged from the burrow.

'Oh, Wilbur, Wilf, I was so worried, thank goodness I've found you!' I blurted, genuinely glad to see my prittleleaping playmates. 'Whatever happened?'

It turned out that my canine concerns were utterly justified.

'The stinky giant and his b-b-bogeybuck came back,' stammered a fearful-eyed Wilbur. 'It was teatime. Daddy and Mummy took us for a picnic. We were about to tuck in to mummy's hawthorn brownies when… they… c-c-chased us…' Wilbur trailed off.

'Are Mummy and Daddy OK?' I asked gently, a magpie-shaped well of fear draining into my seething stomach.

My woebegone dynamos nodded, and a shuddering Wilf helpfully added, 'Daddy lost a bit of his tail trying to drive the monsters away. Mummy's still really scared, she says she won't come out again with that gnashing nasty about.'

At this the traumatised kits burst into fitful sobs and buried their terror-struck faces in my lap for comfort. I tried to stay calm for their sakes and soothingly stroked their velvety ears, but a Bellington-Fraser tempest rampaged through my hopping-mad mind. Was there no end to Hugo's bloodlust? One thing was clear: I had to stop his devilish escapades before it was too late!

'Would you like to go blackberrying?' I proposed, hoping the nosh-based distraction might rally my spirited sprogs.

At this they bucked up and, after I dried their chilling tears with a handy dock leaf, Wilf scuttled off down the burrow to get parental permission for the intrepid expedition. Wilbur passed the time by animatedly informing me of the blackberrying hotspots whilst attempting to vault over a fallen ash tree.

'Daddy says we can go if we stick close to Miss Ella at all times,' Wilf reported diligently, nuzzling his salvaged clover cuddly for added succour. Somewhat bewildered by Mr. Rabbit's trust in my guardianship, we ebulliently bounded off to where Wilbur proudly proclaimed were '...the bestest blackberries in Trolliloes!'

He was spot on and within a few minutes we were contentedly munching the woodland's succulent bounty. Wilbur and Wilf had reverted to full-on hyperactive hare mode, wrestling each other, chasing glistening damselflies and generally trying to outdo each other with shows of bunny bravery.

'Wilbur, Wilf,' I enquired, 'what would you say if there was a way to scare the stinky man and his do... and his bogeybuck away?'

At this the boisterous boys stopped cavorting and sprang over to me, pricking up their downy ears attentively. 'Do you mean there's way to make them go away?' queried Wilf hopefully.

'Yes,' I said confidently, although still not exactly sure of my enticement tactic. 'I've got an idea how to stop this once and for all.'

The endearing scallywags both cheered and broke into a hilariously accurate chant of, 'Stop the smelly stinkweed!'

'But I'll need everyone's help to stop him, you know how stinky he is! Would you tell Mummy, Daddy and all the other rabbits to meet me at the big beech tree, do you know where that is?' They nodded vigorously, bobbing up and down in excitement. '...to meet me at the big beech tree in two moonrises when the sun is at its highest.'

'Beech tree, beech tree!' shrieked my impassioned playfellows, celebrating our inevitable future success with further pawfuls of perfection.

With a bellyful of blackberries and a refound zing in their zip, I dutifully returned Wilbur and Wilf to the safety of their warren and skipped forth to enrol my next animal accomplices.

A glimmer of aureate radiance playing on a patch of gleaming silverweed brought to mind the gladdening golden joydle of Hilaire and Colette. Perhaps their digging prowess could be of assistance in capsizing the big ship Bellington-Fraser. But as I neared the fern-freckled clearing I was alarmed by a fur-frizzling squeal: 'Oh, Hil, it's a calamity, a catastrophe, a *cataclysm*!'

'D-d-do you think we can save her, Col?' answered a choked, het-up voice.

I broke into a sprint, terrified that Hugo's illicit chicanery had blighted another poor family. Rounding the bend I was confronted with an abominable scene. Hilaire and Colette were in floods of tears and hunched over something in the corner of their joydle. Approaching the doting duo, I steeled myself for what might be unearthed. But my overpowering dread only increased as Colette plaintively wailed: 'There's nothing we can do, she's finished!'

I was, however, rather surprised and mightily relieved to find the silver-furred sweethearts keening over a snapped tuffet of yellow archangel.

'Is everyone alright?' I breathlessly asked, just pleased that the engaging gardeners were still alive and kicking.

'Oh, hallo, dear,' sniffed Hilaire, wiping his tear-sodden smoky face with a dusty paw. 'I'm afraid you've caught us at rather a bad moment. Poor Col's had rather a shock, you see. It's OK, darling, we'll make it better,' he added, tenderly caressing his wife's shaking silvery saddle.

As Colette crumbled into another broken-hearted bawl, I surveyed the harrowing scene. The gold-blossomed nirvana, so bewitching and idyllic at my last visit, had been savagely smashed up. Severed stalks, plucked petals and shredded leaves littered the dappled forest floor, the once-beautiful beds had been roughly rumpled and, the final dog-gifted deathblow, was a steaming mound of excrement right at the centre of the gilded utopia.

'What happened?' I requested, eager for the hoary poppets to dish the dirt on barbaric Mr. Badger-Frightener.

'It was that foul whumpstick man and his skeletal hound,' grimaced Colette. 'No whumpstick this time but caught us out in the open at the joydle yesterday. Hil was so brave, fending off the snarling pair as we hotpawed it home. Just made it back in the nick of time. They had a good go at digging us out but eventually sloped off. Thought we'd escaped and then... this!'

With that, Colette descended into another vehement peal of tears.

'Twelve years we've worked on the joydle,' bemoaned Hilaire despairingly, 'and it's all gone in one night!'

I had thought my loathing for Dad's arrogant tormentor could plumb no further depths, but after the bunnies and the badgers my wrath crash-dived all the way to the Challenger Deep. It was only Hilaire's endlessly positive encouragement that dragged me and Colette back up from our gloomy rock bottom. As we broke the sun-kissed surface, they agreed to attend the Hugo-hampering meeting: 'Anything we can do to help, dear,' Colette sniffed, dejectedly clearing a clump of mangled goldenrod.

With the shadows lengthening, I bid the shattered soulmates adieu. Seared onto my retinas forever more would be the sight of my sad joydlers desperately struggling to rebuild their life's work. Flushed with ire, I wished that I could sink into the scrumptious Turkish delight sky.

Leaving the severed serenity of Trolliloes, I half expected to stumble upon the very germ of this evil epidemic, but instead it was his downtrodden drudge who I spied acting shiftily. Hobbling backwards and forwards in front of the Arc-de-Tastelessness was a wizened figure who crouched every now and again to scrabble around by the marble steps. From the size and gait of the fellow, it could only be Mungo Dunthorpe. Using my trusty binoculars, I covertly watched the MD as he traversed the stallionback, getting the distinct impression that he was searching for something.

'Lost anything?' I called, approaching the hunched countryman.

Mungo lurched upright 'Oh, Miss Ella, what a… err… nice surprise. Lost something? Oh… no, no, no, not me.'

'Then why have you been walking back and forth staring at the ground for the best part of ten minutes?' I probed, wondering if a guilty-looking Mungo knew about the peregrine. 'It looks awfully like you're looking for something precious?'

Mungo was clearly no prizewinning poker player and his mouth silently opened and closed a couple of times whilst he furiously fidgeted with his cloth cap. I decided to press further; perhaps Mungo knew of the terrible act?

'I only ask as last week it was here I found the *body* of a peregrine falcon!'

At this, Mungo's face furrowed in agony. 'Oh, missy, no!'

'It was shot,' I added darkly. The words hung in the air like a cloud of midges which Mungo quickly tried to shoo away. 'Shot?' he said with a surprise that fooled no one.

'Yes, shot,' I repeated, deciding to go for the coup de grâce. 'Was it you?'

At this Mungo flopped down heavily and slowly shook his head. He dropped his cap and wrung his fingers through his palms as if trying to cleanse himself of the sin. I could have prolonged the torment, but seeing his benevolent dejected face, my heart instantly melted.

'Fortunately, I rescued the peregrine and we released it in full health this morning!' I proudly declared.

At this Mungo's eyes twinkled as brightly as the obsidian-eyed celebrity itself, a smile creasing across his weathered cheeks. 'Oh, Miss Ella, that's the best news I's heard in weeks!'

I helped the lovable limping lackey to his feet and walked him leisurely back home to the black-and-white borstal of Beggar's Well.

'But if you think Hugo did it, why don't you stop him?' I prodded inquisitively, keen to discern the full dire picture.

'It's not that simple, missy, he's me boss, yer see, and I didn't actually *see* anything,' grunted Mungo, as if condemned to his browbeaten destiny. 'He just comes past me on me rounds with his flashy rifle and that scraggy mutt and a whopping big grin saying he's "*Taken care of some nasty business*".'

'Which was shooting the peregrine!' I hollered, staggered by my own sassiness. 'You could tell the police.'

At this suggestion Mungo gave a resigned titter: 'So, let's say I goes to the police, which I don't say I does but I do. And let's say they listen to an old codger like me, where's the evidence they'll ask? You said yourself, falcon's all better and released.'

'But you could testify against him,' I implored, hoping to win round the ill-starred skivvy.

'My word 'gainst his. And you know a man like Mr. B-F'll have some fancy-pants lawyer. I wouldn't stand a chance and I'd be out a job and a house to boot. Good work ain't easy to come by round here, 'specially at my age,' he explained stoically, his bloodshot eyes wearied from his raptor recce.

'But you must have some evidence of all the other things he's been doing?' I bullishly proceeded.

'Other things?' asked a faux-befuddled Mungo.

'The rabbit coursing and the badger baiting and the buzzard shooting,' I whispered conspiratorially.

'How d'you know about that?' he murmured, glancing warily around for signs of his whipcracking boss.

'So you *do* know!' I answered, triumphant in my dirt disclosure.

Mungo stepped through his rickety monochrome picket gate and closed it firmly behind him.

'Look, Miss, I's said me views, so please leave an old man his sliver of peace before Mr. B-F comes a-trampling,' he pleaded, his energy seemingly being sapped with every choked-up breath.

As he turned for the house, I cried out, 'Wait!', pulling out the dog-eared photo from my shorts pocket. 'What about this?'

Mungo took the faded snap in his withered clod-caked hands and gave it an intense confounded stare, his dark bushy eyebrows rising with every passing second.

'Well… I'll be jiggered!'

## CHAPTER 11

# ELEVEN FOR HEALTH

Without further explanation, Mungo politely opened the scabrous ramshackle gate and hirpled inside Beggar's Well to 'wet the tea'. Returning with a couple of chipped porcelain mugs blotched with faded bucolic scenes and brimming with a rich hazel brew, he motioned I follow him through a dilapidated rose rambled archway.

'I hope you don't mind it strong, we ain't got much milk, yer see,' Mungo apologised, leading me round to his vibrant patch of paradise and a pair of sun-bleached decrepit deckchairs nestled in the corner of the moss-mantled patio.

The colourful contrast to the soulless tumbledown lodge could not have been starker. The lush manicured lawn was swaddled by a scintillating floral bedspread and accentuated by a weeping copper beech as its flaming focal point. Though clearly compact, the vivid haven seemed to extend beyond the honeyed horizon and encompassed all the colours I could imagine, and some I could not. Feathery cerulean speckles of a ceanothus embellished a leaping lemon ligularia, a twinkling tangle of fuchsia fairy lights the resplendent trimming to a variegated lime-green hosta, and to crown it all, rose upon rose upon rose – exhilarating vermilions, blushing apricots and glistening amethysts.

'It's lovely, Mr. Dunthorpe,' I breathed, genuinely astounded by the crumbling abode's eye-catching Eden.

'Ahh, it ain't so much,' murmured Mungo bashfully. 'But me missus loved it, and I now keeps it as she would have wanted.'

'Yer spry, missy,' he added, clinking mugs before taking a thirsty gulp.

Detecting my somewhat perplexed look, he smiled. 'It's what me grand-pappy used to say at toasts, means to yer very good health.'

We savoured the reinvigorating nectar for a few awkward moments, neither one of us quite sure how to proceed. Eventually Mungo pluckily probed, 'That, errr, photo… where'd yer get it?'

Hesitantly at first, I tried to explain the sepia-tinged snap, not wishing to give too much away. But my guard was abruptly dropped by Mungo's simple question, 'How's yer dad?' Before I knew it, the past year's tragic avalanche of trauma came hurtling forcefully from me. It felt immensely cathartic to finally offload my sorrowful cargo, another poke in the piebald chest of my avian abductor. Detailing the precipitous black diamond slope Mum and I had slalomed down, Mungo listened in silence, his gooseberry-green eyes first bulging in anguish, before bursting, tart heartfelt tears gushing down his tanned leathery cheeks.

'So, you see,' I continued, with my own resentful raspberry-red eyes trickling tranquillising juice, 'it means a lot to me to find out anything more about Dad.'

Extracting a large spotted handkerchief from his trouser pocket, the sensitive skivvy gave his dribbling nose a long hard blow and then gazed out at the weeping beech with a nostalgic glint in his rheumy rhubarb-green eyes.

'It were back in the days of the old Earl, Lord rest 'is soul. He was squire round these parts for fifty years or more. You wud've loved the Earl – adored his nature, a real custodian to Socknersh.

I was 'is estate manager, like Pop before me and me grand-pappy before him.

'One summer's day, the Earl comes a-calling to Beggar's Well, trailing a little scrap of a lad. Says the sprog's parents are friends of friends, or summit like that, and he's here for the month whilst they're on business in America. Says the kid loves nature and could the missus and me look after him, yer know, show him round. Well, my Phyllis and I couldn't have been happier. We was never blessed with littl'uns of our own, yer see, and the Earl knew how much we loved to have nippers about.'

Weaving his wistful tale of intrepid adventures, I pictured a lanky countryside-loving dad exploring the vast viridine valley with his Washwell warden. Cocooned within the inspiring contours, there was tree climbing, birding, pond dipping, bug hunting, den building and even nocturnal stake-outs of badger setts!

'You know,' remembered Mungo, 'we even planted a beech tree on the field up yonder – used a mast from the big beech at Trolliloes. It was a fair size before Mr. B-F tore it down for his grand ark, or whatever he calls it. And I think that photo is yer dad and me by the old beech. He loved that tree, so do I, truth be told.'

'Why didn't Dad ever mention coming here?' I asked, keen to comprehend his Arcadian amnesia.

Mungo shook his head sadly: 'Probably too young, yer see. And his parents were likely narked when they found out he'd been hanging about with the likes of me. They imagined he'd be taking dinner with dukes rather than brekkie with a bumpkin. Never let him come back. It broke me Phyllis's heart...'

With his fatherly affable face now a heartbreaking watermelon mush, I diverted the revealing natter to more mirthful memories. However, the trill-bespattered tranquillity and rose-infused fragrance of the rubescent twilight was without warning brutally wrenched away from us.

'*Dunthorpe! Dunthorpe!*' roared an incensed voice. 'Where the devil have you got to, you cretinous half-wit?'

To my dumbfounded horror, storming into Mungo's blissful idyll came the pungent presence of Hugo Blaring-Foghorn, scrawny hound in tow.

'What the *hell* are you doing here, Dunthorpe? Kicking back your feet with some floozy on *my* time!' he snarled, giving me a glacial glare as if I had just served him a cup of steaming manure.

Mungo instantly stiffened, his gnarled hands clasped together in pleading penitence: 'Oh, t-t-terribly sorry, Mr. Bellington-Fraser, sir. I-I-I'd dun me duties for the day and was just having—'

'Your duties?' sneered Hugo malevolently, flouncing back and forth to assert his supremacy. 'How dare you lecture me about *your* duties? *You're* lucky to have a job here, you dribbling moron.'

I sat cringing at this botched pantomime in seething silence. Never before had I actually met the beastly villain of the piece, despite all the times Dad railed against his egocentric captor, so suffering him in all his reptilian depravity was instructive to say the least. In my recent rambles, I'd been at pains to steer clear of Socknersh's King Rat, afraid that he might recognise something of Dad in me, but it quickly became apparent that this odious baddy was so completely and utterly self-obsessed, he would have failed to notice Her Majesty the Queen at Buckingham Palace. Indeed, I began to suspect that he would have been none the wiser if diligent loyal employee Andy Pearson had been toiling away right under his blood-smelling nose.

'And where the blazes is my favourite gun?' Hugo barked, swaggering around like an arrogant murine monarch.

'Your gun, sir?' asked Mungo innocently, flinching at the whiskered would-be overlord.

'Yes, you idiot, my gun, Long Tom.'

'Long Tom?' Mungo winced, slowly rolling the words around his mouth and giving me the distinct impression that he knew exactly where the pathetic pea-shooter was hidden.

'Yes, it's been missing since I shot that f…' Hugo's evil eyes flitted shiftily towards me, '…errr, since I took care of that nasty business up near my magnificent shrine.'

'No, sir, no idea,' mumbled Mungo hastily, shaking his head and recoiling in fear. 'I'll have a look in your gun rack first thing t'morrow.'

'Tonight, Dunthorpe, tonight,' corrected the supercilious slave driver cruelly, before condescendingly inspecting me.

'Miss Ella's just moved in on t'other side of the valley,' explained the kindly fairy godparent, cowering in his seat.

'I don't care if she's the Queen of Sweden, she's—'

'Leaving,' I shot back, wallowing in the imperious pinhead's deflated look as I pilfered his punchline.

Anyway, I couldn't stomach another second of this beastly bully's ranting, and with a burgundy velvet curtain descending on the day's action-packed performance, I needed to get back to Mum. Feeling a piebald pang of trepidation as I brooded over my canine-blighted masterpiece, I desperately hoped her artistic afternoon had been more Monet than Munch. Gratefully escaping through the picket portcullis, I overheard the final snippet of Hugo's me-me-me monologue as Mungo tentatively asked, 'Sir, I wonder if there's summit I might talk to yer about…'

Treading the selfsame burdock-edged bridleways as a young Dad gladdened my healing heart. I imagined my timorous nature champion and his tender tour guide playing Pooh-sticks on the sun-freckled footbridge, just like we had at the real Pooh Bridge. Traversing the poppy-stippled skylark pasture, I visualised him flying a kite and reflected on our windswept downland escapades. I wondered whether to recount the boyhood Washwell gallivanting to Mum but worried that the risk of her subsequently getting wind of our narcissistic neighbour was too great. Besides, Mum's mending mind was undoubtedly a gem-encrusted casket crammed with golden soulmate memories and it was perhaps best I kept this juvenile jewel to myself.

As I reached the Heartsease gate and passed the swooning sylvan bride, I was looking forward to a delectable, with luck, dog-free dinner and a pyjama-clad relax with my reinvigorated heroine. But in the gathering gloam, the lifeless windows of our avocado haven stopped me short. Surely Mum would have switched on the lights by now?

Blocking out the muffled 'I-told-you-so' corvine cackle, I scurried up the driveway as calmly as I could. There had to be an explanation for this, perhaps Mum was in her bedroom categorising her winter wardrobe, or maybe she was relishing an ice-cold lemonade under Dad's emerald oak parasol. With each nerve-shredding scamper, my angst ratcheted up another octave, until it was positively soprano as I gingerly pushed open the back door to locate my leading lady.

'*Surprise!*' squealed a sparky voice.

Anxiety dissolved into relief as the lights flicked on and I was engulfed by an ebullient Mum.

'You're back late, sweetie. Bet you've got some intrepid adventures to tell me all about!' she enthused, squeezing me tightly like she'd genuinely missed my company. The euphoric shock of Mum in such a joyful and uncharacteristically mischievous mood was almost too much to bear and I found myself feeling quite faint. I was completely befuddled when she tantalisingly added, 'And I have two more surprises for you this evening! Close your eyes, darling.'

Mum guided me by the hand for what seemed like an eternity, spinning me around at points to ensure I was totally disorientated. With the full effects of dizziness just about to overwhelm my rumbling stomach, she mercifully stopped and invited me to open my eyes. To my astonishment I was standing in my bedroom, and there, in pride of place on my previously stark wall, was a striking painting of the peregrine!

'Mum!' I gasped, incredulous at my talented dark horse's creative genius. 'Did *you* do that?'

As I inspected the faithful depiction, she turned an abashed shade of Rothko-red. My budding bird portraitist had exquisitely captured our dashing wanderer – the Prussian blue plumage, the proud poise and the effulgent obsidian eyes. It was the perfect souvenir of our tercel sovereign's sojourn!

'I don't know what to say,' I blabbered, embracing my gifted little Gauguin. 'It's stunning!'

Promising 'one final surprise', Mum led me excitedly out to our own teeming Tahitian-esque paradise. The sweltering heat of the day had ebbed away and now the valley's crimson-cloaked contours were drifting into a serene slumber. But Mum's dogless radiant disposition floodlit our sundown saunter. In fact, she was so ablaze with glee that I briefly wondered whether my watercolour wizard had unearthed an old master and was about to announce our *Antiques Roadshow* sky-high valuation.

'Now, I had assumed you'd be home a little earlier,' Mum smiled, arriving at our pristine greyhound-prohibited garden furniture, 'and that it would be a little lighter, but no matter. I wondered if you wanted to have a snack before dinner?'

'A snack?' I repeated slowly, still bewildered as to why this merited Mum's merriment.

But all became clear as she produced two four-finger Kit-Kats. Sandy-toed and ozone-soused, we'd traditionally munched through these melty digits of deliciousness whilst admiring the cobalt-flecked breakers at Banthorpe Cove. But since Dad's indulgence-denying death, these customary seaside snacks had been absent from our canine-controlled shopping trolley, as if the bliss-layered bars were somehow offensive to his memory.

So here was real progress, a sign that her pleasure-spurning pooch was finally being stifled. As we jubilantly feasted on our fingers of chocolate-coated scrumptiousness, I felt a profound sense of peace unknown since those halcyon beach-besotted holidays.

*

'Mademoiselle Ella, so good of you to join us for our latest topographical anatomisation!' trumpeted Piedmont Buteo from his lofty marble pedestal.

Last night's spaghetti carbo-no-row and cheering *Amélie* romp had buoyed me up for today's critter recruitment drive. It finally felt as if Mum and I were much thicker than the soul-snitching thieves who'd invaded our lives. Yes, this newborn buddy-buddy bond was certainly a welcome vitalising revamp of my world, and I hoped that the rebuilding project would continue.

This morning, leaving my creative sister-in-arms scouting the internet for future art explorations, I'd hiked intently up to the stallionback on the hunt for committed game fair saboteurs. With my aural superpower primed, I was delighted to have caught the bookish buzzards in full highfalutin flow, hoping this would aid my smooth-talk assignment.

'As I was saying to my dearest muse and consort, the angular fragmentation constitutes an all-pervading theme of hermetic anarchy. Don't you agree?' interrogated Piedmont, haughtily ruffling his fawn tail feathers.

Entirely in the dark about what Piedmont was yakking on about, but keen to garner his eventual support, I chose my words with utmost care: 'Yes.'

'Yes?' catechised a rapier-like Demelza, looking as if I had stolidly suggested the decongestant properties of swallowing a pinecone. 'So by inference, do you also agree that the malignant metastasis that scourges our verdant Valhalla prevents a true cenobitic exploration of nirvana?'

The higgledy-piggledy hurricane of words gave me a mind-numbing migraine. Why did these blathering birdbrains never make any sense? Discerning my vulgar confusion, Piedmont flapped his brindled wings as if to take flight, casting me a supercilious glare before whispering something to an equally donnish Demelza. As she nodded, I feared that I'd forever lost the chance to convince them of my cause. I muttered the cryptic cipher over and over to myself, hopelessly attempting to get the gist of the cerebral gobbledygook. Oh, all this buteonine la-di-da balderdash was such utter folly… That's it, the *folly*!

'I completely agree with your wise assertion that the monstrous architecture and dark smear of the folly upon the wonderful Washwell Valley make it nigh on impossible to fully appreciate the landscape,' I briskly stated, crossing my fingers that it was sufficiently swanky to make the grade.

At this the erudite academics' beady eyes twinkled and Piedmont gratifyingly raved, 'Ahhhh, a fellow aesthete! May I offer my sincerest *amende honorable*, I have gravely misjudged your stratospheric sagacity.'

Having won, or at least not lost, this round of buzzard flapdoodle, I swiftly pressed home my advantage: 'Piedmont, Demelza, I wonder if I could speak with you about a matter of the greatest urgency and discretion.'

Flattery got me everywhere and I was quickly joined on the ground by the profound pair.

'Tell us, dear lady,' breathed Piedmont conspiratorially. 'Our beaks shall be sealed.'

Summoning my inner Shakespeare, I spelled out the omnipresent peril: 'To be or not to be, that is the question. As you are well aware, the Washwell faces an existential threat. A force so callous and malevolent that it will stop at nothing until each and every Washwellite is visited by the ominous and fearful owl of death.'

'You mean the tweeded sable-haired seigneur of the château?' spluttered a flustered Demelza.

'The butcher of Valentino!' snorted Piedmont acrimoniously.

'The very same.' I nodded, privately pleased with their reactions. 'As I'm sure you both know, cowards die many times before their deaths; the valiant never taste of death but once.'

My criminal quoting had the desired effect and, as we parted, Piedmont and Demelza offered me their 'wholehearted and undying fidelity'.

I strode forth into the head-soothing serenity of Trolliloes and reviewed my apparent enrolment successes. Thus far it had been relatively easy to persuade my animal allies to attend the meeting. Of course, it helped that the bunnies, badgers and buzzards had all been directly dirtied by Socknersh's feculent stain. But I pondered whether swaying the frivolous deer and foolish pheasants would be such child's play. The cervine fidget-rumps were probably completely clueless about Hugo's grand venison ploy, and the farcical pheasants appeared to be barely cognisant at all, let alone aware that they would all be killed. But given my feverish desire to make the gun-greedy ogre eat humble pie, I reckoned it was worth a shot.

My fears were well founded as I came upon Orion and Albemarle gluttonously grazing on a bed of indigo bugle. They considered my welfare concerns to be hilariously misplaced. When I tried to expound the dangers of being captured, penned and slaughtered, they rolled about in fits of uncontrollable laughter. The mirth only subsided when Ori remembered she was wearing a fetching new quad of sky-blue harebell hoofbling, and took great pleasure in detailing the epic chronicle of their purchase. Infantile giggles restarted when she coyly admitted that none other than the archstag of Sussex had thrown her hoof bijouterie an admiring glance or two.

Desperate to quell the chortling couple, I finally plumped for bribery and hinted that there would be a veritable mountain of mouthwatering munchies at the meeting. Dispiritingly, this did the trick, and so keen did they become that they even vowed to tempt Messrs Bucker, McEndoe and the archstag himself to enjoy the foliar banquet. Departing on strangely good terms, I despaired for my naive cervine friends – they literally had no idea of Hugo's devious designs on their haunches.

Leaving the warmth-dappled wooded wonderland, I headed for Pheasant Field. Fortunately, it was all quiet on the Hugo front, and the gallinacean dimwits had helpfully gathered in a garrulous gaggle at the far end of the field. A quick glance through my binoculars suggested the purposeless presence of chairpheasant Strumpwaffle at the heart of the crazy kerfuffle. As close to a leader as I could hope for with this bouquet of blockheads, I aimed to talk round the harridan hen, stressing their impending doom in a bid to brainwash the rest of the baffled birds.

But my efforts at pheasant diplomacy fell on deaf ear tufts. As I approached, the nebulous swarm scarpered, zwerping hither and krabfoodling thither with noisy abandon.

'Frau Strumpwaffle!' I called out impatiently, trying to attract the attention of the führer pheasant. 'Frau Strumpwaffle, can I have a word?'

Startled to hear me chanting their idol's name, the whole daft posse wheeled as one and flocked around my legs. A wall of scatty tumult enveloped me, making it impossible to think. Then, with remarkable coordination, the befuddled flock skedaddled and Frau Strumpwaffle advanced.

'Frau Strumpwaffle,' I began, incredulous that I was about to inveigle the screwy superior.

'Please, Fräulein, call me Strumpy, all the best pheasants do!' was the unexpectedly amiable response.

'Errr, Strumpy,' I continued nervously, 'do you like living here?' It sounded so utterly trite, but I wanted to start simple in case I overwhelmed her.

'Ja,' clanged the unpromising reply. At this, the other pheasant automatons irritatingly launched into a monotonous chorus of, 'Ja! Ja! Ja!'

'And are you excited about performing in front of your philanthropic providers?' I ventured, sprinkling a touch of captivating razzle-dazzle.

'Ja.'

This was going nowhere fast and, resigning myself to complete failure, I tried one last question: 'You don't worry that their explosive praise might get a bit, well, too explosive?'

At this there was a deathly hush. After the deafening pandemonium, the complete stillness was somewhat uncomfortable. All eyes were now fixed on me. I wondered if I'd said the wrong thing. Some fearless pheasants began muttering, others neurotically pecked up stray morsels of grain and a few stragglers diffidently zwerped in discomfiture. But the unnerving silence was smashed as Frau Strumpwaffle bossily bawled, 'Right, everyone back to work! I'll accept nothing but krabfoodle faultlessness when I return!'

The addled horde scrammed in every direction. With all this thunderous brouhaha, I barely heard a hushed, 'Follow me.' Turning, I saw Frau Strumpwaffle jerking her umber-speckled head towards the edge of the field. I trailed the scuttering hen, unsure of why this warranted a woman-to-woman powwow.

As we reached the hawthorn-hemmed perimeter, Frau Strumpwaffle deftly slipped through a hole in the mesh fencing, hurriedly zig-zagging onwards to the crest of the hill. Having negotiated the derelict stile, I joined the rapt hen to appreciate the bosky whale-backed Washwell from her picturesque perch.

Now released from her shackling prison, the high and mighty head pheasant was transformed, stretching her mottled wings, fanning out her tail feathers and gulping in deep lungfuls of dropping odour-free air. With a thankful glint in her enigmatic eyes, she proclaimed, 'It's beautiful, isn't it?'

I was flabbergasted; was there more to this blustering bird than met the eye?

'I come here every evening, just as the sun is setting, and each time I marvel at our sublime valley. See the way the trees cascade down the slopes, like a verdant waterfall tumbling into the revitalising river. Truly it is heaven.'

'But I thought...' I spluttered, bemused by her profundity.

'Fräulein, I see how you look at us,' she snapped, shooting me a withering glance. 'It's how all the animals look at us. Perhaps you think we are idiotic blatherskites – feathery dunderheads who deserve our lead-shot fate?'

'I had no idea,' I replied, still nonplussed by this unforeseen wisdom.

'Of course you didn't, no one does. We are immediately judged on our gaudy guise and rowdy racket,' Frau Strumpwaffle sighed forlornly, pecking at an unlucky grasshopper.

'I'm sorry, I won't make that mistake again,' I apologised. 'So you know about what... err, happens with a pheasant shoot?'

'Some do,' she answered sadly. 'And it is our job to prepare the others.'

'Prepare?'

'Imagine if you discovered your sole reason for existing was that rich men found your death *amusing*,' she lamented, hanging her shrewd head in despondency. 'What would you do?'

I pondered the question, before replying, 'I would try to escape.'

'Ahhh, how very human, convinced that your own intellectual superiority offers the way out. Of course, some *do* try to fly the coop – you see their corpses littering the countryside, a morbid reminder that we pheasants are only here to die.'

'Our way is different: we accept we cannot safely abscond; instead we give the others, the ones who don't know, a reason for living.'

'The dance competition!' I hollered, tittering at the thought of Justin in full krabfoodling farcicality.

'Ja, it gives them meaning in their brief lives. When the end comes, as it always will, they meet death joyfully, zwerping their hearts out.'

I respected her calm determination, and although the logic seemed alien to me, she clearly cared deeply about her feathered friends.

'Strumpy, if there was a way to stop the shooting, would you help?'

'Fräulein, I have heard all about your plans.'

'Heard?' I gasped, stunned at how fast tyrant-toppling tittle-tattle travelled.

'Ja, your badger confidants mentioned it when they dropped by for some dandelion-leaf salad yesterday evening.' She smiled, revelling a little in my surprise. 'I am prepared to help, but heed my word of warning! I assume in your plans it is not *you* who will be in danger? Remember, no animal will risk its life for a song; you will need to present us with a shotgun-proof reason to gain our help.'

At this she spun on her claws and yelled at her confused compatriots, 'Form a line, I expect first-class zwerping perfection, or they'll be no grain tonight!'

With Strumpy reuniting with her muddled menagerie, I started for home to the disappointing drone of black-and-white doubts whirling through my mind. Despite the day's small victories, I felt utterly deflated – tomorrow, when the animals heard my plan was purely glorified Hugo humiliation, they'd run a mile. Observing a shivering small copper trapped in a wasp spider's gossamer ambush, I empathised with its grim, irremediable predicament.

Craving a friendly face, I paused by the shambly Beggar's Well. But all was alarmingly quiet. I was about to traipse on when a signal of promise distracted my gaze. Hopeful it was Mungo, I was miffed that any movement was merely the front door quivering in the breeze.

'Mungo?' I called, anticipating another cordial encounter with Dad's warm-hearted ranger.

No response came, and as the wind picked up, the door swung slightly open. The exploited poodle must have forgotten to close it in his standard Hugo-induced hurry-scurry, so I pushed through the gate to perform my good deed for the day.

Gripping the tarnished brass handle, I shuddered as a turbulent draught eerily moaned through the doorway. As I started to shut the rotting blistered door, something tripped its black splintery foot. I froze, my own raspy breath exacerbating the tempestuous breeze. And then I clapped my terror-stricken eyes on it – a shadowy mass in the desolate darkness of the other side. I tried forcing the geriatric door open, but something blocked my way, something heavy. Feeling a flash of piebald panic rocket up my throat, I put my shoulder to the rickety wheel and heaved. To my sheer horror, there, prostrate on the parquet, was Mungo Dunthorpe.

CHAPTER 12

# TWELVE FOR WEALTH

Administering Mungo the steaming sweet tonic, I gazed gravely upon his battered countenance.

At first the amiable countryman had refused to speak, let alone admit anything was amiss. Eventually he had nonchalantly muttered, 'Leave me alone, missy. Just a silly old fool tripping on 'is doorstep. I'll be a'right now.'

But we both knew that a mere sill could not have meted out a slit chin, multiple rainbow-hued bruises and a gruesome black eye. Thanks to the scrumpled box of Elastoplast in my rucksack, I cleaned and dressed the lurid wound and applied a tea towel of frozen peas to the inky orb. Perching on the grimy parquet, I'd stubbornly refused to leave until the mute minion had come clean.

Following several frustrating minutes of sipping silence, I abruptly stood, threatening to report the lethal step to Mungo's murderous whipcracking boss.

'No, Ella, please don't do that,' he begged, wringing his weather-beaten hands apprehensively.

'Then tell me what happened,' I implored, desperate to

wheedle the truth out of the, quite literally, downtrodden doormat.

The cup now drained beyond the dregs, Mungo had nowhere to hide.

'It were just after yer left,' he groaned, wincing as he struggled to move his agonising mangled mouth. 'All that talk of the old days had gone to me 'ead. Thought I'd take the squire to task for all the, yer know, all the nastiness he's been up to. Stupid, really. Not sure what I was expecting.'

My frosty, rage-numbed heart thawed at the image of soft-centred Mungo attempting to reason with that vile everlasting gobstopper. Had diligent Dad ever tried spouting off and been confronted with a similarly violent sulphurous geyser?

'It didn't go well?' I prompted.

'No, he took very unkindly to it. Don't think he's used to others yattering back. Went the colour of one of me radishes and next thing I knows, I'm on me hall floor with you shaking me shoulder.'

'I'm so sorry,' I morosely mumbled, my corvine tormentor inflicting guilt-racked jabs to my ribs.

'Sorry? What've yer got to be sorry about?' queried a fuzzy Mungo.

'It was my fault. I encouraged you…' I repented.

At this the considerate drudge looked at me very sternly. 'Now you look 'ere, Miss Ella, yer words were the scrummiest pick-me-up for an old bumpkin like me. I's been kidding meself about Mr. B-F, turning a blind eye to all his bloody schemes. It was right and proper I said what I said. The only thing I should have done different is said it years ago!'

With Mungo too now cognitively clobbering himself for his perceived culpability, he leaked the full extent of Hugo's bloodlust. My hunch on the deer's haunches was concerningly correct – Hugo planned to pen my tennis-mad mates straight after his pompous pageant. He'd also made covert local enquiries to purchase a terrier 'for baiting'. And, to my utter horror, Mungo hinted that the introduction of leporine strangleeye lurgy was no accident.

Assuming our confessional was at an end, I was intrigued when he added, 'Anyways, I knows the real reason the squire's all rucked up.'

'Real reason?' I repeated, impatient for him to dish the despot-dirt.

'Yeah, he's been all of a tiswoz these past months 'cos of summit else. Course, he thinks I'm too derpy to understand, he forgets I used to manage the Earl's estate accounts. I knows a wrong'un when I sees it.'

'What do you mean?' I enquired, still perplexed at what the benevolent lackey meant.

'Mr. B-F likes to pretend he's all high and mighty, yer know, richer than Her Majesty. But the Queen don't need to be on the blower to her bank pleading for more time to pay. And, from what I 'ear, his Crapstone business ain't doing so well these past few months.'

At this I felt a tiny seed of comfort sprout from the sorrow of Dad's death. Could it be that without their star skivvy Hugo's infernal consultancy was struggling?

'That's why he's up to all these moneymaking plots, yer know, like them poor pheasants and that daft game fair.'

'The game fair?' I innocently quizzed.

'Yeah, his final throw of the dice. Could be all over if that don't work out for him.'

The ruinous revelation was a soaring skylark to my tempestuous mind. My ingenious stratagem had a chance! Not just to deflate the puffed-up pustule, but to terminate his stewardship of Socknersh forever.

'Anyways, missy, it's getting late,' muttered a jaded Mungo. 'Yer mum'll be worried 'bout yer!' He struggled to his weary, buffeted feet. 'I'm OK now, well, as OK as I can be. Ain't nothing more you can do for me tonight.'

As I bid farewell to my bashed-but-not-beaten confidant, he took my hand in his wrinkled mitt and gratefully uttered, 'Miss Ella, thanks for everything, you've really helped me.'

After the reeling despair of earlier, I now felt gleefully giddy as I gambolled home. Not only was there an opportunity to rescue my fellow Washwellites, but I could also stop Dad's slave driver in his fetid tracks. Letting out a contemptuous corvine cackle, *I* taunted my own pied persecutor: 'Who's laughing now?' The malicious magpie, like all bullies, had become refreshingly absent in the face of my increasing confidence.

As I strode up the final field, the valley itself seemed to mirror my ameliorating mood – a clamorous kettle of swallows whistled in the cirrus-wisped sky, their midnight-blue wings applauding the evaporating vermilion sun. Blissfully shaded by the beech-ceilinged sunken track, the mirthful whirr of a hummingbird hawk-moth further raised my spirits as it delicately twirled on its blushing valerian dance floor. And could that sinuous burnt sienna flicker scurrying into the fern fringing be a hunting stoat?

Bounding euphorically down the Heartsease hallway, my potato-pining nostrils were instantly enraptured by the redolent long-lost scent of a roast dinner. Surely not? In a ravenous heartbeat, I was transported back to Elysian Sunday evenings, the three of us high on fresh-air adventures and hungry for seemingly endless stacks of spuds. Back then there was always time for seconds. But our tattie tuck-ins had abruptly ceased three years ago when Dad's weekends had become more about angst-infused PowerPoint presentations than empyrean roasties.

'Is that you, sweetie?' called a chirpy-sounding Mum. 'Better hurry, I'm just dishing up!'

I was in succulent seventh heaven once again as I rounded the tater-fragranced corner and found Mum ladling hot onion gravy atop groaning platefuls of roast beef ambrosia.

*

Sated by a Bastille-storming revolutionary breakfast of croissants and *chocolat chaud*, I'd charged eagerly into the ravishing coup-rousing contours of the Washwell as they awaited my mass movement's watershed rebellion. But my creature-led crusade could only triumph if my Animal General Meeting was first a recruit-convincing victory. Saddled with a glutted rucksack of garden-harvested deer snacks, I skipped defiantly along the insurgence-championing footpaths. What a corvine-free contrast to the magpie-molested yomp of my first valley expedition! And now my greyhound-grappling responsibilities were less pressing too. Earlier, my exultant little skylark had excitedly exclaimed that Kate was *returning* for a girly day out tomorrow – I let this little white lie pass! What a perfect anarchy-abetting arrangement – Mum on a Kate-accompanied coastal art safari whilst I led the Washwell Resistance at the game fair!

Preparations for the Bellington-Fraser jamboree were in full grandiose swing as I prowled around Socknersh's gilded perimeter. Bewildered alpacas and astounded alligators watched on as the ostentation offensive's combat zone was transformed. A strident troop of bawling jackboot-sporting mercenaries was erecting a growing barracks of khaki tents, encircled by a regiment of livestock pens, fenced show rings and gunmetal grandstands. And the crowning bluebottle on this faecal festival was a massive presentation stage, overlooked by a titanic big screen.

Wow, Hugo really was going all out to defibrillate his dying dukedom dream! It was even more monstrous than I had imagined, more like a macabre military theme park than a country fête, and must have cost a pretty penny to build. Closing my eyes, I envisaged all the tyrant-chastening chaos that my ballsy band of riled rebels could stir up. And I finally knew exactly how to return the spud-swindling laptop. Now all I needed was my own patriotic army!

As the scorching sun conquered its Everestian summit, I sweated it out under the lucent cool of my ear-enlivening beech.

Toxic toothed tuffets of dog's mercury encroached upon my kicking heels and a fluttering seville-stippled fritillary proved an indifferent coach to my fraught preparations.

As the minutes tiptoed by with no animal attendees, I began to panic that it had all simply been a beguiling magpie-generated mirage. But just as I was about to throw in the Socknersh-splatting sponge, an inspiriting, if somewhat discordant, caterwaul drifted from the underscrub. Canoodling through the nettles, ambled the affable striped faces of Hilaire and Colette.

'Sorry we're late, dear,' apologised a puffed-out Colette. 'Got halfway here and then Hil remembered he'd left his best bracken neatly folded on the nuzzlenest. Had to rush back to sort it out!'

Not wanting to enquire about what exactly a badger would be doing with his 'best bracken', I was at once gladdened to spot Wilbur, Wilf and a twitchy beige buck bounding into the brindled clearing.

'Hi, Miss Ella, we're ready to chase away that nasty bogeybuck and his smelly man!' squeaked an ever-lively Wilbur, jumping on Wilf's back to confirm his dedication.

'Ooof! Daddy, tell Wilby to get his paws off me,' protested a squished Wilf with a disgruntled look on his elfin fawn face.

Ignoring his quarrelling sons, the daddy buck hopped over and bowed graciously to me, politely introducing himself as Willard. Next to arrive were Piedmont and Demelza, lustily keeyodeling through the sun-kissed canopy.

'Dear lady, a thousand regrets for our temporal tardiness,' gushed an ever-incomprehensible Piedmont. 'The chimes slithered through our corporal consciousness like a weasel in a waterspout.'

Puzzling over this latest Mensa edition of buteonine buffoonery, I was heartened to see Orion, Albemarle, Bucker, McEndoe and the archstag himself frolicking into the erudite action. Unfortunately this hopeful highpoint was swiftly dashed as the archstag, his magnificent antlers accentuated with a trendy floral tinsel of ultramarine brooklime, lemony silverweed and diamanté daisies, took a decidedly disgusted look at the other unadorned recruits. Having haughtily paraded along his cranesbill-carpeted catwalk, this vain fashionista eventually parked himself alongside the mountain of plant-based munchies, his vacant gaze fixed on Orion's handsome hoofbling. Fierce rivals Bucker and McEndoe, meanwhile, irately eyeballed each other, glaring so fixedly at their foes that I was extremely glad there was not a pinecone in sight!

I held back a few more minutes, fretfully awaiting Frau Strumpwaffle's arrival, but with the deer having almost polished off all of my leafy nibbles, I was forced to commence my eager exhortation.

'Thank you all for coming,' I started, rather haltingly. 'I've been most touched by how kind and welcoming you've all been to me.'

Murmurs of appreciation scurried around the kaleidoscopic clearing, only to be chased away by a derisive archstag snort: 'I don't have all day, *two-leg*, get to the point or I'm orrff.'

Hoping my revolutionary rhetoric would win over the stubborn cervine-dominated crowd, I raved, 'We are lucky to live in the most perfect, beautiful valley one could possibly imagine. Since the moment I came here, you and it have lodged deep within my heart.'

Reassuring nods of agreement rippled through the stormy sea of spectators, only to crash harshly on the intransigent cervine rocks.

'But we all face a bloodthirsty threat – a hostile force so dark and determined it will stop at nothing until you are all dead!'

To a harrowing accompaniment of leporine wails, Colette's distressed sobs, and dismayed mutters of 'Blackguard!' from Demelza and Piedmont, I candidly detailed Hugo's menacing master plan.

Concluding my rebellion-kindling diatribe, I paused to allow the animals a chance to consider the calamitous crisis. To my surprise, the arrogant archstag tore himself away from his Chinese bean blossom canapés and flounced onto the mossy main stage. I had hoped he might add his considerable weight to proceedings, but when I saw his condescending apathetic expression, I knew that I had failed.

'I have never in all my born days heard such a far-fetched fantasy,' he bellowed, swanking about on the dappled dais. 'This is utter rot and poppycock! I have wasted good skittingling time to listen to this two-leg's ridiculous ranting.'

The sneering stag hurled a wrathful glare towards a belittled Albemarle and Orion, before kicking off a fierce denunciation of my attention-diverting tactic.

'Do you *seriously* suggest that a mere two-leg could ever outskittingle the archstag? Ha, the thought itself is laughable!'

'Your grace,' I implored, for how does one address an archstag? 'What I say is the truth: you and your herd are in grave peril.'

'Peril? The only peril is listening to *your* dangerous delusions. Perhaps it is *you* who is the harbinger of doom, sent to poison the virtuous minds of us valley folk? Why, I have a good mind to order my bucks to run you out of—'

The hoity-toity stag's dissenting soliloquy was abruptly broken off by the meteoric crash-landing of Frau Strumpwaffle. Cannoning right into the flabbergasted glimmer-mottled glade, she rounded upon the bombastic bad boy, jabbing an accusatory wing in his direction. 'You fool, you flower-headed fool!'

From the look on the swaggering renegade's muzzle he had never been spoken to in quite such a manner.

'We pheasants were once like you – so blinded by our own vanity that we never saw the two-legged danger. Now look at us! Short, miserable lives ended by man's trigger-happy malady. Mark my words, stag, *your* fate will be as good as sealed.'

The seething archstag bristled, furiously pawing the unyielding earth with his restless fore hooves.

'Archstag,' entreated Piedmont from his regal beech throne, 'the lady is the Washwell Oracle, veracity made flesh. My venerated compeer Valentino has passed through nature to eternity on account of that Mephistophelian murderer!'

'Poor Uncle Kelvin died from strangleeye lurgy just last month,' snivelled Wilbur, looking most down in the whiskers. 'No one's ever caught it before,' added a whimpering Wilf.

'And my joydle is all but destroyed because of that insensitive savage and his gimlet-eyed beast,' urged a cut-up lachrymose Colette.

'*You* will be next, archstag,' beseeched a bullish Frau Strumpwaffle. 'Don't let your pride get in the way of the truth. Don't become like us pheasants!'

The archstag stroppily tossed his knockout antlers through the branches of an overhanging birch, sending a multicoloured flurry of wildflowers swirling to the ground. 'We are leaving,' he imperiously hissed, turning on his livid hooves.

'Wait!' squealed a valiant female voice.

To my sisterhood-supporting astonishment, blocking the archstag's exit was a stout-hearted Orion.

'Apollo,' she purred, batting her long eyelashes in his direction, 'what if Ella is right? What will we do if we can't skittingle our way out?'

'But Ori,' Apollo blustered, peacocking swankily along his rutted runway, 'it's madness, nothing like this has ever happened before—'

'But life's like the seasons,' she ploughed on, 'always changing. And for every season we must wear the chicest hoofbling. I fear with your obstinacy we are about to make a fatal fashion faux-pas. And of course, you mustn't forget the fast-approaching rut.'

'The rut?' queried a baffled Apollo.

'Yes, Polly,' melted a flirtatious Orion, tickling his toffee-snout with a twitch of her tail and mesmerising the blushing buck with her dark doe eyes, 'the rut is so close and you wouldn't want anything to get in the way of your *performance.*'

'Ahhh,' grunted Apollo, 'that does put… errr… a rather different spin on things… errr… Carry on, two-leg!'

'Her name is Ella,' Ori gently reproached.

'Carry on, *Ella,*' muttered a humbled Apollo, settling himself back down beside the remnants of my bloom-based bites.

Still winded from the archstag's snide intervention, I rattled through the game fair set-up, Hugo's perilous finances and ultimately, my devious subversion strategy. My animal allies listened in silence, the cervine crunching of rosebuds the only punctuation to my persuasive politics.

'So if this all works,' enquired Willard, 'will the gun-wielding maniac disappear forever?'

'There's a chance he will leave,' I answered honestly, hoping that it wouldn't be the nail in the coffin of my Hugo annihilation bid.

'Chance?' queried Colette anxiously. 'Is it worth the risk?'

'The greater risk, my dear badger,' suggested Piedmont, 'is that in risking nothing, we lose it all. If *we* do not act, then others will.'

A harmonious chorus of assent reverberated around the irradiated cyclamen-festooned rostrum. Placing our hooves, paws, claws and hand into the centre of the sun-streaked stage, we swore an unbreakable oath of defiance. The revolution would commence at twelve o'clock sharp tomorrow.

Brimming with rabble-rousing verve, I sprang sparkily home, the promised end of Dad's relaxation-robber enlivening each and every sanguine stride. With Mum also marshalling her own canine uprising, felicity fizzed through my grateful veins. But emanating from the diamond-fissured trunk of a silky goat willow sapling, came a rather more melancholy mewl. Approaching the tree, I was shocked to find the gangly frame of Roly St. Clare wedged against its gnarled toes and bawling into his salmon-shirted sleeve.

'Roly?' I ventured, dismayed to find him looking even more

wretched than on our last heart-rending encounter.

At the sound of my voice, his face jerked up in surprise and he sheepishly ruffled his boyish blond hair in a failed attempt to affect normality.

'Oh, sorry, Ella, isn't it? Just taking a moment for myself in the evening sunshine before I get back on it – sheep shearing tonight, you see,' he sniffed, seemingly as discombobulated as his edgy jumper-clad ewes.

'Is everything OK?' I asked courteously, sensing that it unfortunately wasn't.

'Tell you the truth, no,' he gulped, panting in the sultry dusk. 'Been trying to keep up a brave face for Harriet dearest – poor lady's almost due and I don't want to worry her. In fact she has no idea what's going to happen. Frightful mess! Beastly shame!'

'I'm sorry to hear that,' I offered, the insincerity of my bland condolence grating my ears. 'Can I help?'

'I wish. It's that Mr. Bumbling-Farmnerd… umm, sorry, Mr. Bellington-Fraser,' he hastily corrected. 'The blighter's quadrupled the rent and threatened to evict us in a fortnight if I don't pay up. I've nowhere to go, and with Harriet…' Roly tailed off, this Lost Sheep's pitiful plight strangling any further words.

Fishing around in my pocket for a bleat-lulling tissue, I pulled out Wilbur's dock leaf. It reminded me that even in the depths of despair, joy was only a prickleball away.

'Roly, however bad it feels, there is *always* hope. Why don't you come to the game fair? It might give you space to think,' I suggested.

Leaving the forlorn farmer quizzically cradling the withered dock leaf, I hiked hurriedly back to Heartsease, keen to share the luscious raspberry ripple sky with my born-again ice cream addict. But I found Mum in somewhat of a pied pickle.

'It's this rug, sweetie,' my reinvigorated gelato gourmet explained, motioning to the black-and-white abomination which dominated the lounge. 'If you'll pardon the expression, it's been eating away at me ever since we unfurled it. To tell you the truth I hate it, I really hate it! It was a present from Dad's cousin Margot, you remember Margot?'

I shuddered, how could I forget! But it was cheering to see Mum's sense of humour returning and her acknowledgement that she was ill.

'Dad insisted we lay it in the old lounge, but only because the daft old bat had schlepped it all the way back from Dubai and he didn't want to hurt her feelings, bless him.'

It was as if the labyrinthine designs of the obnoxious monochrome monstrosity were smirking up at us from the dusty floor. Mum was right, it was insufferable, just like my magpie menace.

'Mum, you know how Dad always did what other people wanted,' I suggested, proffering a guilt-absolving Get Out of Jail Free card. 'Did he ever say *he* liked the rug?'

Mum puzzled for a moment. 'No, I can't remember him ever saying so.' Then she smiled impishly. 'Darling, you're a genius! Shall we...'

'...chuck it?'

'Yes!' she sang out, delighted at this permission to free herself of the contemptible encumbrance.

And then it came to me, a chance to give Mum's now-unwanted stray a final rehoming:

'Mum, why don't we give it to that greyhound rescue charity down towards the coast? Those dogs could probably use a repulsive rug to curl up on.'

Mum grinned: 'What a great idea! I could drop it off tomorrow with Kate on our way to the Jerwood Gallery. At least it would make one poor dog's life a little richer. Although, to tell you the truth, I've never much liked greyhounds!'

## CHAPTER 13

# THIRTEEN BEWARE IT'S THE DEVIL HIMSELF

The dawn sky's apoplectic pink glower presaged a tempestuous day ahead. Instead of pirouetting sunlight-ballerinas, an incandescent flock of scarlet-fleeced sheep rampaged across the contours of my duvet. With luck, my lost-souled Washwell herd were ready to rise up against their massacre-bent rustler. On tyrant-toppling tenterhooks, I yearned for some jubilant avian encouragement, but was deafened by the nerve-riddled rasps of my own ardent breath. Would my Dad-inspired shepherding mission be a game-changing success? And could my dedicated drove pull the wool over the lamb chop-loving lord of the manor's demonic eyes?

'You're quiet this morning,' observed Mum shrewdly, pouring herself a bowl of golden-clustered granola.

Whilst finger-licking fry-ups and gold-top garnished cereal were a way off, I was grateful that the 'how many handfuls' hoo-has of past months had been fizzling out. Munching through my raisin-studded rabbit food, I hoped the rebellious bunnies were in high spirits for our ogre-ousting offensive.

'Are you sure you don't want to come with me and Kate? First we're dropping by the Jerwood, and then we're on to Eastbourne to check out the Towner Gallery!' she enthused, scattering her brimming bowlful with succulent blackberries. 'We're hoping to round off the trip at Fusciardi's ice cream parlour. Dad used to take me there when we were courting, you know. Jaffa cake was my favourite flavour!'

'No thanks, Mum,' I answered, thinking of my berry-gobbling cervine saboteurs as she tucked in to her fruit-flecked feast. Would they deign to join our Capstone-crumbling crusade after the arrogant archstag's dissenting snorts? 'This day is just for you. Don't worry about me, I've got a few things planned to keep me out of mischief!' I joked.

'Well, take a coat, love, the weather forecast mentioned thunderstorms this afternoon,' she warned.

Savouring the last spoonfuls of my putsch-powering petit déjeuner, I hoped against Hugo-humiliating hope that the wet weather wouldn't hinder our ego-bruising blitz.

I was mightily relieved to see a zestful Kate pull into the driveway – a tiny part of me had wondered if Mum's amusement-impeding mutt would snarl back – and helped load the repellent rug into the car boot, ready for its new canine home. Joshing with her fellow aesthete as they pulled out of the driveway, Mum was the picture of contentment. Greyhound willing, their jaunt would be more Seurat's *Grande Jatte* than stormy Turner seascape. With them en route to exhibition heaven, I set to work.

Whilst anarchists might be satisfied with a mere cookbook, all revolutionaries need a rucksack. I primed mine with my assault armaments: a Hugo-razing howitzer in the guise of Dad's laptop, my trusty binoculars for covert surveillance operations, my battledress of waterproof jacket and Mum's wide-brimmed sombrero as cunning camouflage, and, last but not least, a water bottle – because even dissidents get thirsty!

Pulling on my combat boots, I marched forth into the lead-vaulted Washwell, on the warpath to defeat Emperor Bonaparte-Fraser. A humid suspense-saturated haze infiltrated the victory-spurring valley and bludgeoned the sweat from my forehead. As I reached the game fair, sweaty but not browbeaten, a louring range of Himalayan cumulonimbus glared down at me, their churning satanic spires providing a foreboding canopy to my looming onslaught.

At the ominous entrance to Hades stood a khaki garrison, policed by a militia of tangerine T-shirted conscripts. Socknersh's official security force, whom I instantly christened the SOS squad, was summoning up its inner Titanic spirit to steer Hugo's ill-fated festival around any pride-sinking icebergs. I desperately longed for our obstacle-creating operations to leave Captain B-F crying out in undignified distress.

Joining a long queue of bored locals, I spied more jackbooted soldiers patrolling the perimeter railings. Surely these upstanding punters weren't handing over their hard-earned cash for a jolly at a prisoner-of-war camp?

Entering the tent, I was frisked for my £18 – my protestations of childhood dismissed with a curt 'over 5s pay adult fee!' – and ordered to join a new line. The money was secured in several steel strongboxes, viciously guarded by a Cerberus of snarling Rottweilers. These groaning treasure chests represented cash-hungry Hugo's salvation from banking damnation. If my discrediting tactics were to triumph, I had to liberate the loot!

'Inspection!' roared a belligerent voice.

'Err… sorry?' I asked, quizzically gawping at the orange-attired hothead who now beckoned me over.

'Baggage inspection!' he sharply clarified.

Stalactites of angst stabbed through my veins. 'You've failed!' chortled my pied tormentor, finally awakening from its joy-induced slumber. 'Just wait till he finds the laptop…'

The SOS officer wrenched my backpack from me and commenced his brutal interrogation. After ransacking my rucksack, he cocked his head towards his walkie-talkied shoulder and muttered: 'Sir, we have a situation, code crimson, repeat, *code crimson*.'

Petrified at the thought of my 'code crimson' punishment, a callous clementine-clad commander strode towards me. His servile lackey pointed into my dubious holdall and Colonel Cruel donned a pair of red rubber gloves to conduct his own intimate examination.

Extricating his prying gauntlets, he stared fixedly at my terrified face: 'You are in possession of illegal contraband! How do you plead?'

'P-p-plead?' I stammered, panic-stricken by this unexpected intrusion. How could I have been so stupid – of course they would be conducting bag checks!

'You have obviously come here with malevolent intent, attempting to selfishly subvert a happy family event. True? Answer the question!' he bawled.

'I-I-I don't know what you mean,' I blustered, desperately playing for more time.

'Then how do you explain this?'

At this, the sour citrus-garbed colonel roughly thrust his gloved hands into my private property and extracted… my water bottle!

I stifled a derisive snigger as he bitterly berated me for: '…attempting to circumvent the purchase of high-quality beverages.' How very Hugo – more intent on milking the locals for moolah than visitor well-being.

Finally released from my aqua-triggered internment, and with my illicit item deposited into a luminous yellow bin marked '*Hazardous Waste*', I surveyed the battlefield. Meandering mirthful throngs of gelato-licking families trundled in and out of the mousy marquees – would Mum's priggish greyhound be prohibiting her knickerbocker treat? Peeking into the Grand Floral Pavilion, I was genuinely impressed with the Washwell

Horticultural Society's stunning summer display – resplendent sunflowers smiled in unison with aureate auriculas, and dramatic dahlias vied for attention with velvet-petalled lilies – perhaps even Hilaire and Colette might approve?

A distant cheer drew my gaze to the gundog scurries, the arena surrounded by swathes of Labrador-owning country gents, all trying their luck at the tricky course. Down by the turbulent boating lake, a brethren of well-rodded anglers were in solemn communion with the carp population, a jeroboam of champagne the prize for the most impressive catch. Lining Bellington-Fraser-land's Main Street, a fusillade of firearm stores, country clothing boutiques, leather saddlers and enticing eateries each tried to tempt the gullible guests to part with their guineas. In pride of place on the avenue of excess rotated the hog roast, Hogzilla himself giving up his life so that the ravenous rabble could feast.

But it was to the presentation stage that I headed, keen to charge my laptop thunderbolt. There I found *him* swanking around with the county's glitterati, securely penned in an elevated decking area awash with bubbly and the rank stench of entitlement. Inadvisedly dressed in stifling tweed, Hugo was attempting to play the benevolent country squire. In a drastic bid to ennoble his vainglorious head, he wore a blood-red fedora accessorised with pheasant-feather antennae, projecting skywards like the horns of Lucifer himself.

Approaching the Vastly Inept Plonkers, I caught the fetid whiff of boastful banter: 'As I was saying to the German Chancellor, "*Mr. Chancellor, sir, you're going to need to shave that poodle if you ever want to—*"'

'But Hugo, daaarrrling,' interrupted a chandelier of a lady, dripping in diamonds, 'isn't the German Chancellor called Angela Merkel?'

This stumped an egg-faced Old Nick and sparkly solitaire eventually had to clarify: 'You know, a lady?'

'Ahhh,' blustered a winded Hugo, 'well… this chap was definitely chancellor of something.'

Behind this pathetic performance I noticed the big screen flashily announcing: *The Honourable Hugo Bellington-Fraser will be giving an address at 12pm. A complementary beer is available for all those who attend!*

*Honourable?!* Since when had that disgrace of a man ever had a shred of honour? Like all charlatans, he was desperately disguising his flagrant faults with bombastic fabrications. I skirted around the back of the presentation stage, looking for the electronic source of the big-screen lies. Spotting a lone laptop tantalisingly hooked up to a thick navy cable, I stealthily closed in on my quarry.

'Hey you! No public access!' slurred an inebriated SOS lieutenant, clocking my snooping as he lurched out of the beer tent.

I swiftly diverted towards the falconry grandstand, trying to affect an air of confused nonchalance. My ultimate attack would need a great deal more SOS-bamboozling subterfuge, perhaps with an animal diversion to provide the perfect camouflage.

Talking of animals, I pondered whether my allied army was advancing? Glancing up at the serene safe house of Trolliloes, I ached for a small sign of life, a glimpse that they were ready for insurgent action. But all was dauntingly still. An agonising piebald panic assaulted my throbbing brain – without hugging my enchanted beech and, in any case, being outside of stallionback field, I would be deaf and dumb to my accomplices. What was I to do? What if they needed my help? What if they were in danger? With a stiff corset of fear strangling my chest and tungsten trainers impeding my feet, I heard the clamorous crackle of a loudspeaker. High-principled Hugo was about to sermonise his loyal congregation!

A sizeable crowd had gathered in front of the presentation stage, no doubt bribed by the magnetic promise of free booze.

The billowy leaden peaks of earlier had briefly departed and a scalding oily heat now basted every gristly sinew of Socknersh. Squinting into the searing sunshine and basking in a smattering of underwhelmed applause, our sententious villain strode onto the stage, scraggy greyhound in tow.

'Thank you all for coming,' he prattled, before going on to tediously list his many qualities and 'awe-inspiring' accomplishments. As he was extolling the 'impossible prowess of my self-built company, Capstone Consulting', a dusky shadow fell across the murmuring arena.

Funny, I thought to myself, there was barely a cloud in the sky a moment ago. Looking up, I spotted a violent vortex spiralling above Trolliloes Forest. Lifting my trusty binoculars, I gasped, for it was not droplets of water which furiously swirled and spumed over the ancient woodland, but thousands and thousands of avian anarchists!

Never before had I seen so many species in one place. There were rooks and robins, skylarks and sparrowhawks, ducks and dunnocks, pigeons and pipits, gulls and geese. Seemingly all the birds of Trolliloes were flocking above the forest and at their head, keeyodeling in synchronised ecstasy, were Piedmont and Demelza.

I felt as if in a surreal dream, the beery happy campers all around me totally oblivious to the supernatural events unfolding above. As Mr. Bragging-Fool's speech reached its own tortuous crescendo, the fast approaching trills, squawks and warbles of the super-flock swamped the loudspeaker. Suddenly they were upon us, the feathered air force attacking Hugo and his posh sycophants with pecks, scratches and well-aimed faecal smart bombs. Within seconds, Hugo's 'horns' had been torn off his head and his tweedy outfit was peppered with gloopy guano.

Panicked pandemonium erupted amongst the patrons – men, women and children screamed in terror, bolting hither and thither. Ducking behind the stage to avoid the trampling hordes,

I was instantly reminded of the hapless skittery pheasants. Maybe we weren't so different after all!

As the plumed posse pressed home their attack, people poured under the khaki canvas to escape. Hot on the Hunter-wellied heels of a turdy Hugo, I found myself in the clammy, BO- and yeast-infused atmosphere of the beer tent. After a curt command from Captain Conceited, a carrot-topped squaddie briskly secured the flaps. For the moment at least, we were safe.

The screeching din outside subsided, and now in the protection of the perspiring pavilion, Hugo and the crowd relaxed. I even heard some tentative laughter. But all of a sudden the frenzied nipping started. Above our heads the fearsome sound of a thousand beaks beat down upon the swaying wigwam. As the first needle-sharp bills lanced through the roof, and the masses screamed blue murder, I smugly watched as wimpish Hugo cowered under a trestle table. Titanic spirit indeed!

'They're gonna break through!' hollered one man, channelling his inner disaster movie character.

'Has anyone got a gun?' gabbled another.

'Sssshhh,' hushed a petite blonde woman. 'If we don't make any noise, they'll think we've gone.'

The mob immediately fell silent, only its ragged breaths audible. At this, the jabbing incursion swiftly ceased. Our very own little Jane Goodall, emboldened by her apparent mastery of natural history, then exasperatingly sneered: 'Animals are *very* stupid, you know!'

In response, a heavy thump to my left wobbled the whole tent, then another to my right shook the sweltering structure again.

'Are they trying to fly through the flaps?' rattled Hugo from inside his trestled fort.

The SOS bootlicker was despatched to investigate and, gingerly reaching under the flaps, returned with a large wooden spike.

'What's that?' asked our budding animal behaviourist, her zoological genius not extending to basic carpentry.

The tangerine trooper puzzled at the object for a moment: 'It looks like a tent peg. I wonder where it's come from?'

The answer helpfully arrived seconds later as the central supporting column, a totem pole of solid spruce majestically holding the yurt aloft, first wobbled before gracefully toppling to the ground, pole axing poor Jane No-Good-at-All in the process. This was promptly followed by the rest of the canvas as it collapsed in a holey heap upon us.

With the rest of the garrulous gaggle, I crawled on my hands and knees to escape our flattened wigwam and emerged into a shattered world. Lying limply on the scorched earth, each and every tarpaulin fortress had suffered the same fate. A pair of quickly absconding silvery rumps, burying themselves under the prone folds, the only hint of our meline saboteurs.

After their stellar Hitchcock-style performance, the bold birds were now generously augmenting Hugo's horticultural dung heap, alongside redecorating the monstrous mansion in the distinct colour of kak. The mercenary Field Marshal B-F, meanwhile, had cautiously scrabbled out of his timber citadel and was busy bawling orders at his SOS grunts: 'Get these tents back up, block the gates, no one can leave! Keep the cash... I mean, keep the guests here!'

Just then, Hugo's beady-eyed hellhound gave a wolfish howl. This was answered by a flurry of reverberant barks and excitable yaps from around the vast grounds. Soon it seemed like every canine in the valley was baying. Their mystified owners, still shell-shocked from the avian invasion, looked at each other in disbelief.

'What the devil's wrong with you?' growled Hugo as his girdled hollow-cheeked greyhound strained at its leash, yanking the would-be host with the most off his feet.

Before you could say 'sit!', a raging torrent of rabbits inundated the arena. The daft dogs went berserk, breaking free of their befuddled humans and bounding after the barrelling bunnies. Canine chaos ensued, and here, there and everywhere out-of-control owners were levelled by their manic mutts. Passing the ferret racing stand, I couldn't help smirking as I saw Wilbur and Wilf frisking at full tilt, joggletailing away from a demented dachshund as easily as I would outrun a snail.

But icicles of anxiety pulsed through me as Hugo's beastly bogeybuck, finally free of its haughty handler, latched on to their tails. Both bunnies twisted left and right, trying to shake off the raw-boned pooch, but, molded by millennia of human breeding, the wily greyhound was as nimble as a racehorse, and mercilessly hunted down the playful pair. Helplessly back in my grisly rabbit-coursing nightmare, I gave chase, shouting at the top of my voice to unnerve the skeletal beast. The scrawny savage hurtled closer and closer to my furry rascals, its teeth gnashing within a whisker of their snowy scuts. It was too close and I was too slow, corvine convulsions clenched my mortified mind – how could I have let this happen?

From the caliginous clouds above, a celestial shaft of blue steel lanced downward, scoring the bogeybuck's back. With an anguished yelp of pain, the greyhound dived away from my daring duo. The jagged fork stooped again and again, turning impossible angles with each scintillating thunderbolt. I gasped in veneration – it was the peregrine; my sublime knight in hematite armour had returned!

The fulgent-eyed falcon bedevilled the scraggy ogre, harrying the hound until its back bled. Its agile limbs now galloped in fright, the pestilent pooch attempting to flee my avenging archangel. Catching a final reverential glimpse as they charged past the boating lake, the tenacious tercel doggedly drove away the fleshly embodiment of Mum's despair.

Turning back towards the 'shaken but not stirred' arena, I watched aghast as Blofeld-Fraser's Seville-vested infantry regrouped. Despite all the damage, and the legions of rattled dog owners streaming out of the gruesome gala, the tents were being erected once more, and our cock of the walk was back on the presentation stage, revelling in the attention.

'Ladies and gentlemen,' he roared into the microphone, 'apologies for the… errr… interruption, you know how things are in the countryside. Rest assured, we have everything back and running and your tickets are still—'

All of a sudden, a curious faint whirring noise began tickling my eardrums. At first as soft as floating spring blossom, it spooled up like a jet engine until it completely drowned out the strutting dimwit. As it rose to a plume-raising screech, the hysterical audience darted back towards the hazel hideouts.

'What now…' groaned an agitated Hugo, staring at the sinister sky with barely disguised fear.

Catapulting over the gilded Curly Wurly bars with an emphatic 'Krab-a-foodle-doo!' exploded Frau Strumpwaffle and her platoon of cacophonous pheasants. Landing with surprising grace – I wondered if the über-pheasant had drilled them in descent – they set to work zwerping and krabfoodling to terrifying effect. At the bizarre sight of the gallinacean gang, Hugo tried to hotfoot it back to the alcoholic reassurance of the lager lounge. But in his haste, he tripped on the stage steps and bellyflopped into the choppy sea of pheasants. Dance mistress Strumpwaffle mercilessly critiqued the diabolical swan-dive, viciously jabbing the pungent nincompoop with her discerning beak until he scrabbled into the tepee, screaming, 'Get those blasted birds out of here!'

Now I took my chance; with the SOS permatan privates fully occupied failing to round up the gallinacean guerrillas, I sprinted around the back of the stage and hooked up Dad's laptop – the Hugo-razing revolution would now be televised!

My electronic infiltration complete, I contentedly surveyed the crazed scene. The valiant air defence, still piloted by commodore Piedmont and wing commander Demelza, were now wheeling around a band of intimidated anglers who had inadvertently rowed out to the duck house. The rebellious bunnies and badgers had vanished, but so too had every canine visitor. The farcical dance troupe was causing an almighty headache for the distressed SOS officers, the apricot-apparelled lackeys shooing the pheasants away to limited success. Indeed, many were now perched on top of the piebald alpacas, who had somehow escaped their enclosure and were indulging in some gourmet grub. All that was left was…

'*What the blazes!*'

The livid yell could only mean one thing – Hugo had discovered my little parting gift. Strolling smugly round to drink in his enraged expression, I found the self-satisfied laptop slave driver, now emerged from his boozy bunker, staring foam-mouthed at the floodlit big-screen.

*Love*             *Imagination*

*Andy Pearson*
*1974–2019*

*Kindness*             *Humility*

I had to admit, my tribute to Dad did look rather splendid. His broad, beaming smile illuminated the Bellington-Fraser battleground like a brilliant Flanders poppy. Dad might not have been a thrusting businessman with an imposing country estate and his own peach-uniformed security, but he was loved, dearly loved, by me and Mum. In forty-five years he had brought more joy to the world than a whole king-sized kaleidoscope of flitterblossoms.

'*You!*' boomed Mr. Bloody-Furious, pointing an accusing finger at me. 'You, Emma, or whatever you're called, you've—'

For the third time that day, his spittle-flecked sound-off was interrupted, this time by a thunderous bellow emanating from Trolliloes. As Hugo gawked up with a hint of perspiring Pavlovian terror moistening his forehead, I peeked through my binoculars to lap up the next compelling animal onslaught. Lined up across stallionback field was a dramatic cervine armada – bucks, does and fawns in unity – and at the herd's helm, his antlers aptly garbed in vivid bloody crane's bill, was Fleet Admiral Apollo!

At the sound of the archstag's guttural holler, the deer skittingled helter-skelter down the hill, their pelting hooves barely touching the desiccated turf. Leaping the ornate railings as easily as I would mount a step, the cervine tsunami engulfed the game fair. Pinecones went flying as Bucker and McEndoe unleashed a frenzied rally of forceful forehorns and brisk backhorns upon the panicked visitors. This risible riot of antlers sent the feral throngs careening in all directions. Captain Blackbeard-Fraser needed no second hint and, dodging a hail of spruce shuttlecocks, raced back to his hoppy hunting ground, shouting, 'Get rid of them!'

The epicurean deer swiftly set to work on the game fair delectables, gorging through the Grand Floral Pavilion, before moving on to the flashy formal parterre. The alligator topiary was retrimmed into bucktoothed beavers, the fluorescent bedding tastefully remodelled into a leafy-green labyrinth, and the repugnant trellis aviary converted into useful tinder.

Smouldering with complacent success, a battalion of bright orange SOS soldiers counter-charged, waving and shouting blue-murder. The skittish deer took flight, zipping around the parkland before retreating over the Stalag's barricade to Trolliloes.

With the rank miasma of Field Marshal B-F's victory in the air, the jaffa-shirts next set to work on the irrepressible pheasants and defiant birds, clapping their hands and blowing air horns to scatter the rumbustious flocks. As the last wingbeat of Piedmont crested Trolliloes, the game furore was once again silent.

Our Bellington-Fraser blitz had backfired! Despite all the turmoil, the majority of the confused crowd had not left, the wonga-winning wigwams were back up and, apart from a few gardening improvements and a new sludgy suit for Hugo, nothing had changed. I knew my ears would soon be boxed by the incendiary taunts of my piebald dissenter. But nothing came. Instead, looking up at the big-screen with my superstar idol smiling down at me, I finally felt at grief-disentangling peace. I and my masterly band of merry friends had tried our best to stop the iron-fisted Sheriff of Socknersh. Today it hadn't been enough, but our freedom fight wouldn't cease until we thwarted him.

With a depraved cackle, a baker's dozen of magpies burst forth above the big screen. The marauding mob circled over my head, lapis lazuli tails glaring in the blistering sun, then apathetically flapped off, disappearing from view as they passed over the revolting manor house.

'Thirteen, beware it's the devil himself!' exclaimed an affable voice behind me. Turning, I was delighted to find my genial general hobbling over.

'Mungo!' I called. 'How are you?'

'As spry as a scutty, miss, and no mistake,' he responded, a cheerful grin creasing his black and blue face. 'Just got back from a spot of business, actually. Oh, talking of *him*…'

Mungo pointed as the pungent prat finally left his hoppy stronghold and swaggered to the stage.

'Ladies and gentlemen, sincere apologies once again for the strange happenings of the past hour. But like I always say, man will forever have dominion over nature,' he gloated. 'Titanic spirit will prevail—'

The triumph-trumpeting speech was suddenly swamped by a resonant rumble which rolled around the shattered estate. Groaning like Mum's deprived tummy over these past months, the portentous thunder amplified and accelerated, the shrivelled earth began shaking, and Hugo gripped the lectern in fright. Like a shot, a black-and-white cascade erupted forth from the rear of the stage, knocking the odious orator to the ground.

Mungo and I dived for cover as a colossal herd of Friesian cattle stampeded through. Tents were trampled, fencing flattened and grandstands smashed. The crowd, scandalised by the whole utter travesty, were sick and tired, and scampered for the exits. Mixed in with the visitors were the SOS, scared witless by the bovine raid and running for their lives.

As I helped Mungo to his feet, Roly St. Clare nonchalantly jogged past.

'Oh, Miss Ella, what a terrible mess!' he puffed. 'Gosh, the number of times I told Hugo to fix that wonky gate. Now look what's happened!' And as he skipped off to round up his lowing girls he gave me and Mungo a mischievous wink.

In front of us grovelled the pathetic figure of Hugo. His tweeds were ripped and ruined, his hair mucky and matted, his hideous headgear and loathsome hound lost forever. Now more *Lord of the Flies* than lord of the manor, he raised his piggish head and looked daggers at me. He was about to speak, when two pairs of perfectly polished black boots appeared either side of him.

'Hugo Bellington-Fraser?'

'Yes,' he snapped, looking up at the questioner.

'I'm arresting you on suspicion of…'

## Chapter 14

# The bird flies

L ike a legion of avenging archangels, the dawn's Tartarean sky-peaks triumphantly returned to cleanse the befouled squalor of Socknersh. As the police officers cuffed and dragged away a ranting Hugo, runnels of rain first dribbled, then surged down from the blackened billowing slopes, flash-flooding the remains of the fair. Thanking my lucky stars – and omniscient Mum – I hastily pulled on my jacket, bade a cordial farewell to Mungo and splashed ecstatically home.

By the next day, the disinfecting deluge, mixed with a sparkling scoopful of Dunthorpe diligence, had washed the field clean, such that the Socknersh Scandalfest might merely have been a surreal Daliesque dream. The first downpours of autumn, or perhaps the last of summer, had left the sun-baked valley as fresh and fragrant as a warm French baguette. But fully excising the recuperating Washwell's very own malignant tumour had taken rather longer…

Bellington-Fraser was charged with a long list of heinous offences, chief of which was the grievous bodily harm he had administered to his ailing MD. The police's initial source of suspicion turned out to be a gem-laden treasure trove of evidence, handed over by our humble hobbling hero on the morning of the gloat gala – emails, photographs, letters and memos. The imperious pinhead had seemingly never considered his acts to be criminal so had brazenly documented every blemish of his filthy business.

As their investigation deepened, the Sussex constabulary discovered an untapped spring of truth spurting from former Capstone employees, all having received brutal treatment at the hands of their Chief Exploitative Officer. The biggest surprise of all was Dad's laptop – confiscated at the game fair – which coughed up a thick sputum of spiteful, harassing emails, further corroborating the prosecution's case. Despite Hugo's 'fancy-pants lawyer', the guilty verdict was unanimous for each and every execrable indictment. A five-year prison sentence and a £20,000 fine felt like measly recompense for his Argos catalogue of nefarious crimes.

Notwithstanding the best efforts of a vampiric crisis management agency, Count Bloodsucker-Fraser had failed to keep the toxic trial out of the national newspapers – *Captain Capstone sunk by titanic abuse claims* was my personal favourite headline. Reporters camped outside the narcissistic château for weeks on end, trying to dredge up more sulphurous sludge. With Mungo keeping a very low profile, and the badgers and bunnies refusing to give interviews, they soon turned their attention to Capstone's gleaming head office, flashily situated a forehorn's fling from Buckingham Palace.

With a never-ending baggage carousel of negative news revolving Hugo's illicit paraphernalia, one by one Capstone clients cut their ties. Contracts were not renewed, new business was lost and staff rapidly resigned. On the very day that the tycoon of iniquity celebrated his first night behind bars, his corrupt company filed for administration.

The fate of Socknersh was no less revelatory. With the

detained would-be duke having defaulted on months of mortgage payments, and thousands of pounds in personal debt, the bank repossessed the estate. I could sense the viridine valley's susurrant sighs of relief when the National Trust announced its purchase of the conspicuous mansion due to: '*Its critical importance to the nation, the manor house comprising an unusual mix of neoclassical, rococo and gothic architecture; and the wider parkland encompassing arguably the most outstanding landscape in the Sussex High Weald, including a significant number of rare wildflowers and butterflies*'.

I was buoyed up further when I ran into the good ship Dunthorpe a few weeks later, his back a little straighter, his hobbling now less pronounced and the garish facial wounds all healed. He was dressed in a dapper National Trust uniform and clearly in his nature-knowledgeable element showing a grinning throng of visitors around the grounds.

'They've only gone and made me estate general manager, missy, can yer believe it?!' he excitedly whispered to me as the astounded horde gasped at the breaching whale-back vista from Trolliloes.

With Mungo now the new genial squire, Roly St. Clare's extortionate rent was immediately slashed and the farmhouse renovated. Re-energised by this sudden transformative regime change, the endearing farmer proposed converting Glydwish to an organic venture, an idea which was warmly embraced by his amenable boss.

'It's the funniest thing,' Roly later admitted to me, 'I got the idea watching my old girls galloping round the game fair. Good thing someone suggested I go!' he added with a puckish wink.

The rescued ram's euphoria was further cemented when Harriet gave birth to a beautiful baby girl.

'We've called her Primrose,' Harriet explained proudly one evening, showing me the cherubic copper-haired tot, 'because even after the coldest winters, primroses bloom to give us hope.'

Hope. A word that a few months ago was entirely foreign to me. The sanative Washwell had been my living lifeline, bringing cognitive calm and remedial merriment to my bottomless abyss of anguish. With my little skylark launching into her own ebollimento exaltation, Hugo languishing at Her Majesty's pleasure, and the estate and its effusive creatures under the sedulous stewardship of Mungo, my Sussex symphony had truly reached its crescendoing coda.

Except it wasn't quite over, for there was one last inconceivable revelation secreted within the valley's viridian corkscrew curls…

*

Three days after the game fair, when the Washwell's peridot patchwork had finally wrung itself dry, Mum and I were in a reflective mood. Reflecting, that is, on her latest masterpiece – a Cézannesque portrait of our departed naturalist hero.

'It's so like him, Mum,' I gushed, so glad that she could now rejoice in an activity which wasn't an energy-sapping penance. 'You've even captured the warmth in his eyes!'

'You're too kind, my lovely, it's not even finished yet! Although,' she added with a bashful giggle, 'I am rather proud of the eyes.'

The impressionist painting would take pride of place overlooking our lounge, so that Dad would be beside us for every hopeful step of our Heartsease journey. Mum had started this labour of love the day after her tercel triumph, and day by day she had lovingly caressed the canvas with her delicate brushstrokes, each assiduous addition expressing the very essence of what made our beloved idol so wonderful.

With the flamboyant tour de force almost finished, she sought my audience: 'Ella…' said Mum, suddenly looking more *Whistler's Mother* than *Mona Lisa*.

'Yes, Mum?'

'I just wanted to thank you.'

'Thank me?' I enquired, imagining what merited this gratitude – so often had I felt completely helpless in the fearsome face of Mum's guileful greyhound. 'For what?'

'For guiding me back to the right path,' she answered, putting down her paintbrush and looking into her soulmate's dreamy eyes. Her voice quivered, and I sensed she had been considering her next few words for a long time.

'I now know I was in a *really* dark place, much darker than I ever realised,' she forlornly admitted, tears pricking her brilliant burnt umber orbs. 'There were times I went out when I… I… didn't want to come back, times I wished I could keep running… But you… you saved me.'

'Mum,' I choked, the intense emotion of the moment saturating my pooch-parched body, 'you would have done exactly the same for me.'

Under Dad's ethereal presence, and with valiant rivulets of brine now sousing both our cheeks, we tightly hugged, her still-chiselled shoulders a stark reminder of how close I came to losing her.

When we finally dried our gritty grief-exfoliated eyes, I suggested a visit to the GP might be a little overdue. Mum unexpectedly agreed and proposed the same treatment for me, both of us resolving to never again let our lives become so perilous. To honour this empathetic epiphany, Mum found one of Dad's favourite Motown albums and we shimmied and swung our way through the whole blissful joyathon, baptising our newly rug-liberated space as our dedicated dance floor.

Afterwards, whilst my recovering virtuoso made her final careful additions to Dad's memory, I skipped twinkle-toed back out into nature's rapturous rhythm. A crimson-bibbed robin performed a jolly jig on the sun-caramelised plaits of its beech hedge dancehall. Attempting a more manic breakdance, a silver-freckled squirrel spiralled up the lacy petticoats of our sylvan bride. In spite of the late August day, a freshening breeze tousled the brittle heat-scorched trees, dislodging the first auric entries to autumn's colourful canvas. My ringleted slumberer now clung to her emerald eiderdown less tightly, moving her bronzed limbs in time with the wind's mellifluous lilt.

Reaching the lustre-lobed lookout tower of Dad's protective oak, I quietly recited Mum's bird box inscription to rekindle something of his spirit. Despite having barely visited Heartsease, his memory so much infused our little Arcadia that it almost felt as if he *was* here with us. Touching the toughened tortoise-skin bark, I was suddenly compelled to say a prayer of thanks. Kneeling before Dad's shimmering shrine, I closed my eyes and whispered my grateful devotion.

Without realising it, my unvoiced veneration escaped me, and I breathed a most tender and heartfelt, 'Dad.'

'My little Ele.'

Like a cognitive krabfoodle, my mind was jolted by these startling, deeply emotive words. Was this merely a cruel aural mirage, or a garrulous serotinal gust? Still, what was the harm in answering?

'Dad?' I ventured, still not daring to dash the illusion by opening my eyes.

'Lovely afternoon for exploring, hey?'

Surely this wasn't just blustering flimflam? Convinced my acoustic oasis would vanish before my keening ears, I plucked up the courage to take a peek. Wind-triggered will-o'-the-wisp it was then, as my dispirited eyes grieved for the dad that wasn't there.

'I'm up here!'

The eager voice came from somewhere above me, and rang out as clearly as a St. Paul's full peal. I looked up, now totally bewildered. There, perched on a rugged branch throne and observing me with its inquisitive iridescent eyes, was a peregrine.

And not just any peregrine, *the* peregrine – the faded smudge of ochre was unmistakeable.

'Dad?' I asked, feeling as faint as a lycra-clad, food-starved Mum. 'Is that you?'

'Yep, it's me. Bet you didn't see that one coming, did you?'

'But… how?'

'Well, you didn't think I would come back as a leech, did you?' he chuckled, and flew down to join me.

All of a sudden, I was hit by a Daedalean domino run of raw emotion. Coming back round – for I had collapsed at this non-chimera onto the petrichor-charged turf – multiple clamouring questions jostled on my tongue, but only one broke free: 'Why didn't you speak to me sooner?'

He shifted uneasily on his claws and hung his moustachioed head: 'I was afraid,' he mumbled, seemingly ashamed of the very words. 'Perhaps that seems daft now…'

He halted, his remorseful eyes branded with torment: 'Day after day I watched you. I could see how much you were hurting. I desperately wanted to comfort you, tell you I was alright, that everything would be OK…' He trailed off for a few seconds, ruffling his Prussian blue pinions in distress.

'And Mum as well. I followed her mindless marathons, for mile after dreadful mile, as she descended the path I had been forced to take. I wished that *I* could bear the blows of the unseen whip that drove her on, that *my* back would smart with her pain. With each punishing stride, I felt ever more desolate. Do you know what it is like to feel so helpless?'

I nodded, the Beachy Head precipice she'd hurtled towards painfully lodged in my then-powerless head.

'Oh, how I agonised about intervening.' He grimaced. 'But I was afraid. Afraid *I* would make it even worse. And then…'

His scintillating eyes blinded me with a radiant beam of overwhelming love: 'I may be blessed with wings, but it is *you* who is the angel! *You* saved Mum, *you* gently guided her back to the land of the living. *You* stood up to beastly Hugo, *you* stopped his wickedness and saved the animals of the Washwell. It is *you* who I am so very, very proud of.'

This fulgent flare of sentiment irradiated my every smitten cell. Drawing his hematite plumes to my pounding chest, I tenderly embraced him, drenching his ermine cape with my fervent tears. Ensconced in a Baloo-bear hug of yore, we contemplated our own luxuriant jungle. With a brackish River Wainganga rushing down my cheeks, I told him how not a day passed when I did not think about him.

Our miraculous moment together seemed to transcend time itself, and I was somewhat surprised that the moon had not deigned to join my star as I released my doting clasp. A dodgem ride of thoughts bumped around in my brimming brain, but with a flap of his flight feathers, Dad excitedly announced, 'Tonight, Ele, the world is *ours* to explore. Are you ready for an intrepid adventure?'

In a piggybacking role reversal, my velvety hero alighted on my shoulder and we scurried past the sun-steeped sanctuary of our family home. Through the windows, I could just make out Mum, brush in hand, concentration etched on her brow. I feared she might spot our peregrination, but so transfixed was she with the last details of her loyal depiction, we passed unnoticed.

'It's a great likeness,' Dad commented, giving my head a fatherly stroke with a glinting sun-stippled wing. 'If you find a way, please tell Mum I really love it!'

The reinvigorated valley had a novel bustle about it that late afternoon, perhaps anticipating a Hugo-free future. Celebrating our passage with an amber ticker-tape parade, the oak archway revelled in gusty agitation as it liberated flurries of desiccated leaves. A gregarious parliament of rooks flitted above us, riding the eventide zephyr en route to a field de-worming session. Dad cheerfully called up in a language I did not recognise, and they replied and wheeled as one to mark the momentous occasion. This hospitable welcome continued with every soothing step – birds, beasts and bugs all seemed to rejoice in our journey.

Approaching Trolliloes Forest, I was startled to hear a deep, rhythmic thrumming, rising and falling with the scudding air currents. Despite my best interrogation efforts, Dad encouraged me to find out for myself, choosing to button his reserved beak. On reaching the gigantic fern-fringed gates, the hubbub suddenly subsided, replaced with a soft swish, like the retreating surf at Banthorpe Cove. A step or two in, and the forest was hushed, every gnarled root and kaleidoscopic leaf permeated with the absolute quiet of Centre Court in July – both human and cervine versions.

'*Three cheers for Ella!*'

Entering the beech clearing, I was assaulted by a wall of riotous applause as animals of all furs and feathers burst out of the undergrowth to serenade my arrival.

'Miss Ella!' squealed Wilbur and Wilf, breaking ranks from the rainbow of life and charging towards me to hug a leg each.

'A hundred thousand welcomes. I could weep and I could laugh, I am light and heavy. Welcome!' raved Piedmont, keeyodeling from somewhere high up in the coruscating canopy.

'The saviour of Washwell!' cried Frau Strumpwaffle, chirpily leprechaun-kicking in my direction. 'Pheasants, zwerp number 5, go!'

Her gallinacean gaggle erupted into a beguiling group dance greeting, careering about the clearing in a barely coordinated caper that was more energy than excellence. Still, it would have been churlish not to applaud, and I did so heartily.

'Come and see what we've done!' piped Wilbur, streaking off to give me the whirlwind tour.

The entire glimmering glade was decked out for an extravagant party, with lemony bunting bespangling the bushes, violet lanterns beaming from the boughs, peachy picnic blankets spread across the floor and, to top it all off, an entire khaki tent, perfectly erected by some enterprising creature.

Secreted under the canvas was the most elaborate spread of game fair cuisine – fine cheeses of all scents, delectable hams, mountains of leafy salad, intricately iced cakes, heaving heaps of fruit, towering jellies, and bowlfuls of strawberries and cream. The epicurean animals were all making fast work of the gastronomic feast, and with my VIP welcome now complete, the singing and dancing began.

'I hope you don't mind.' Hilaire chuckled, as he sauntered over, following a rocking rendition of 'Back in Black and White'. 'We took the liberty of, err... *borrowing* a few small items from the fair!'

'Oh, you should have seen him last night,' chattered Colette, rubbing the big boar's silvery saddle. 'Hil was getting all grubbed up trying to raise that silly tent. Almost took his claw off in the process! I don't think I've heard so many grumbles since last Yule morning when he had to build our Geneviève her Wendy sett.'

'And that's not all we borrowed.' Hilaire winked, with a playful look in his amiable eyes. 'Come and see the joydle!'

Rounding the rampion-fringed corner, I gasped in sheer amazement. Their ruined garden was once again resplendent in every imaginable shade of yellow from canary through to butterscotch. There were beaming helianthuses, trumpeting hemerocallises, delicate irises, jolly rudbeckias, exploding alliums and breathtaking buddleias. All had clearly been filched from the fair; some even had their price tags still attached!

'It's fantastic!' I breathed in admiration, cheekily adding, 'Did you pay cash?'

'Funny you should say that,' said Hilaire darkly. 'Follow me...'

Dad and I were led to a thick tangle of bracken under the

protection of a prickly holly bush. With a flourish, Hilaire pulled back the ferns to reveal a stack of shiny strongboxes!

'You got the money!' I yelled, thrilled that miserly Hugo's villainous masterplan had misfired.

'We thought it was rather important we removed these boxes from that nasty man,' explained a satisfied Colette.

'What would you like us to do with them?' asked Hilaire, scratching his hoary rump on a handy birch trunk.

Looking at the chocked chests, their sides groaning with gravy, I briefly entertained the thought that Mum and I could use them to buy a second home, perhaps overlooking our beloved Banthorpe Cove. A disapproving frown from Dad provided the cold shower to my avarice.

'Bury them!' I briskly declared. 'Make sure no human ever sees them again.'

'Right you are, my dear,' grunted Hilaire, and immediately set to work on the money mausoleum.

Returning to the magical festivities with my idol in tow, I was delighted that Wilbur and Wilf bounded over again to introduce me to Mrs. Rabbit, enjoying her first fresh air since the bogeybuck incident!

'We're so proud of you, Miss Ella,' the doughty doe exclaimed. 'My boys won't stop telling me the story of the fair. How all the dogs in Sussex were chasing after them...'

'And how they escaped certain death with your help,' added Willard, swiftly hopping over and bowing to Dad. 'We shall forever be in your debt, fine sir, thank you!'

With Dad somehow blushing through his fine-boned cheeks, Wilbur and Wilf charged off after a twirling merry-go-round of flitterblossoms, and I found myself summarily appointed as referee to a friendly wheeding match between Piedmont and Frau Strumpwaffle.

'The loser has to krabfoodle with the pheasants,' proclaimed Demelza with a roguish grin.

'You're on!' bawled a mettlesome Strumpy, threateningly eyeballing her intellectual rival and adding, 'I hope you've brushed up on your Kant?!'

Whilst Piedmont racked his buteonine brains to match Strumpy's stupendous sonnet, I spied the deer over by the food hall, cheering on a repeat of the Centre Field finale. Bucker and McEndoe had swiped some real tennis balls from Hugofest's gundog scurries, their good-natured grunts umpired by an enthusiastic Albemarle.

'Ella,' called Alby as the players took a drinks break, 'you haven't seen my sister anywhere, have you?'

A frantic search around the bustling shindig yielded no Orion, but on closer inspection, no deerstalker was required to detect these master elopers. Coyly hidden behind the canvas was a rather besotted Apollo, his antlers twisted in a fetching tangerine T-shirt, trying out his shameless chat-up lines on a demure Ori.

Not wanting to interrupt the love-struck hunts-stag on his amorous quest, Dad and I returned to find Piedmont and Demelza krabfoodling with the best of them.

'I haven't had so much fun since the heady days of Valentino,' gushed Demelza. 'My, these pheasants certainly know how to zwerp a groove!'

'Dear lady, and valiant sir, won't you join us?' called a zealous Piedmont.

So Dad, I and all the other animals joined the pheasants and buzzards in a full Trolliloes zwerp-and-krabfoodle extravaganza, dancing until our feet were weary and the shadows were lengthening.

'I think we need to be getting back,' whispered a jaunty Dad as we broke from Strumpy's latest line-zwerp. 'We wouldn't want Mum to worry about you.'

With so many animals wanting to personally say goodbye, it turned out that leaving the unforgettable soirée took almost as long as being there. Finally, having bid a heartfelt farewell to every last Washwellite and to a tumultuous – 'Three cheers for Ella and Andy!' – we made for Heartsease fizzing with elation.

Ambling contentedly home, we wallowed in a whistle-stop tour of nostalgic memories. For Dad, it was Cornish coastal walks hand in hand with Mum – me, still in nappies, giggling behind him in the back carrier.

'I can still hear the sound of the waves crashing against the granite cliffs, and smell that seaweed-infused aroma,' he mused. 'Once we even spotted a pair of peregrines, wheeling and stooping in the updrafts. If only I'd known back then…'

I responded in kind – red squirrels on Brownsea Island, rockpooling and bodyboarding at spectacular Kellock Point, exploring the dappled, mystical enclosures of the New Forest and windswept summer evening yomps along the South Downs.

We laughed and cried and laughed again at each glistering jewel of glee, our own liquid crystals streaming onto the enlivened fertile earth beneath us. But before I knew it, we were back at our cherished Heartsease. Dad's hunch had been right – the move had transformed our lives beyond all recognition.

The mellow, fast-fading sun steeped our horticultural haven in a balmy, lustrous glow. Aureate rose petals now scattered the front bed and sepia seed pods bespeckled the Chinese bean tree. But there were other dazzling delights to look forward to: blushing crisp apples and burnished Byzantium blackberries for heavenly autumnal crumbles, terracotta pots to be planted with cheering spring bulbs, and an ever-varying harlequin vermicelli of wildflowers.

I tried to invite Dad in, but growing suddenly serious, he suggested we return to the twilight-mottled tranquillity of the oak.

'My time has come to fly,' he explained, staring out into the beatific gloam to hide his melancholia.

'Fly? But… no… you can't go, not now you've returned!' I grieved, barely able to contemplate losing Dad again. 'We could go inside, I'll introduce you to Mum, it'll all be OK—'

'No, my darling Ele,' uttered Dad resolutely, shaking his crestfallen head. 'This is the way it has to be. You and Mum must now follow your own path and I must fly a different one. Perhaps our tracks will cross again one day.'

With a bitter boiled sweet of sorrow choking me up, I implored him to stay, but it lodged deeper at his insistence that it could never work. Feeling unbearably dejected, I wept against his comforting downy chest, not wanting our precious rapport to end.

Nuzzling his ermine-robed frame closer to my aching body, he recalled, 'My fondest recollection, the one I kept back until now, will always be the day I first held you in my arms. You were so small and so perfect – all I could ever want. As the years have passed, you have grown into a sensitive, determined young woman, just like my little skylark. I can't tell you how proud I am of you. I know now that you and Mum are stronger – your journey will be a joyous one.'

He raised up my chin and wiped a tear from my cheek with a gentle flick of his slate wing. For old time's sake, we paused to drink in the winsome world around us: magenta sprinkles of heart-shaped cyclamen confetti, a murmuration of saffron-spotlit starlings and capricious smiles concealed within the cirrus-striated sky.

Staring affectionately into my dewy eyes, he continued, 'Whatever you do, never lose your desire to explore the world! Take good care of our little skylark and help her to soar again. Never stop chasing flitterblossoms, always prickleball down hills and seek the golden joydle within the darkest gloom.'

At this, the breeze stiffened, ruffling his feathers. He gazed out at the valley: 'I must go now, the Washwell is calling me.'

'Will you ever come back?' I asked, clinging longingly to the hope that he might return.

Preening his handsome hematite cape, he plucked a luminous silken plume from his wing and placed it at my tremulous feet.

'Wherever you go, carry this part of me, knowing that I'll be with you for every sublime step of life's intrepid adventure.'

And with a twinkle in his serene obsidian eyes, he soared nobly off into the gold-rippled sunset.